DIARY OF A
LEFT-HANDED
BIRDWATCHER

DIARY
OF A
LEFT-HANDED
BIRDWATCHER

Leonard Nathan

GRAYWOLF PRESS

Publication of this volume is made possible in part by a grant
provided by the Minnesota State Arts Board through an appropriation
by the Minnesota State Legislature, and by a grant from the National
Endowment for the Arts. Significant additional support has
been provided by the Andrew W. Mellon Foundation, the
Lila Wallace–Reader's Digest Fund, the McKnight Foundation,
and other generous contributions from foundations, corporations,
and individuals. Graywolf Press is a member agency of United Arts,
Saint Paul. To these organizations and individuals
who make our work possible, we offer heartfelt thanks.

Published by
Graywolf Press
2402 University Avenue, Suite 203
Saint Paul, Minnesota 55114

Printed in the United States of America.

ISBN 1-55597-250-0

2 4 6 8 9 7 5 3 2 1
First Graywolf Printing, 1996

Library of Congress Card Catalog Number: 96-75788

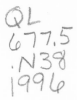
for

Frank Pitelka

and

Jacquelin Pels

ACKNOWLEDGMENTS

Authors know, or ought to know, that their work depends on the help of many others and that any acknowledgment is bound to be incomplete, as is the following, a list of those who so deserve my gratitude: First, Anne Czarniecki, the editor one always hopes for but seldom gets. Then Laurie Saunders, Arthur Quinn, Thomas D'Evelyn, Ted Kooser, Tom Farber, Gary Soto, Russell Schoch, James Larson, Jonathan Holden, Robin and John Gage, Ralph Rader, Mark Osaki, Herlinde Spahr, Anthony and Betsy Dubovsky, Regenia Gagnier, John Dupré, George Hochfield, David Williams, Jim Abernathy, Pat Matsueda, Marvin and Geraldine Nathan, Maxine Fredericksen, the patient young scientists at Palomarin Banding Station, the Tuesday Group, so wise in birds and so generous to (eternal) novices, and finally to Miriam and Carol Nathan.

DIARY OF A
LEFT-HANDED
BIRDWATCHER

THE MASTER SAID,

Little ones, Why is it that none of you study the Songs? *For the* Songs *will help you to incite people's emotions, to observe their feelings, to keep company, to express your grievances. They may be used at home in the service of one's father; abroad, in the service of one's prince. Moreover, they will widen your acquaintance with the names of birds, beasts, plants and trees.*

THE ANALECTS OF CONFUCIUS

WE RISE, SOME OF US A LITTLE SLOWLY. It's after dinner, still light, in Brandon, Manitoba. We have been at it all day, seeking birds, the last few hours of the afternoon in a vain quest for the small and secretive Yellow Rail, *Coturnicops noveboracensis,* according to Peterson's *Field Guide to Western Birds:* "Mouse-like; difficult to see or flush." Now we are about to try again. Our leaders pile us into our bus and head us out once more to the rail's habitat.

The bus comes to a stop on a road through a vast marsh, where we climb out, take off our hiking shoes, pull on our high rubber boots, and stand listening for the telltale *tic-tic tic-tic-tic.* I hear nothing, but both our guides point at what seems like pure distance, then crawl through the fence wires and stride out, we sloshing as fast as we can behind them. As we straggle up to the spot they have chosen, we are instructed to form a loose circle. There are twelve of us in all. The circle, including our leaders, is perhaps twenty feet in diameter, a gap of about five feet between one person and the next.

Is it any wonder that popular opinion regards birdwatchers as a little mad? Here we stand, in the dying light, up to our calves in marsh water. The men of the group are slowly realizing that the thin shirts they wear—it has been unseasonably warm for June—are not going to protect them from the dusk chill. But there is nothing for it. We can't even shift positions, so we stiffen in the ones we hold. We can't because any noise could spook the rail (if it's truly in our circle), and a misstep could tumble us into a soaking hole. So we wait. And stiffen. And wait. Our guides are relentless. We have come to see this bird; by heaven, we are going to see it, even if, at any hint of permission from them, we would gladly slosh back to the bus.

I am, in fact, developing a dislike for the rail. I know the others feel the way I do. I can see it in their faces before night shuts down on us, and can hear it in their soft grumbles and bad jokes. I hear myself softly grumbling and making bad jokes. "Oh, so this is what a Druid circle was like—no wonder it's a dead religion. Ha. Ha."

Meanwhile it gets darker and chillier and mosquitoes have found us, although our guides concede nothing to these trifling inconveniences. We fall silent in the dark, our minds drifting, our eyes following the blue glow of fireflies all around us. A passing patrol car flashes its beam, sees who we are (Druids of a disbelieving age), and passes on. We can imagine the dialogue in the front seat. Then a sudden *tic-tic,* and we wake up cold and alert. A guide calls out to me, "It's in front of you, Leonard. How far?"

"Three feet," I guess.

"All right, we close in slowly, very slowly or it's going to slip through us." We move in step by slow step and begin to join hands. We think we may have it. Closer, closer—but no! The bird is a Houdini of escape. It seems to have slipped between the feet of one of the Druids. The circle breaks and our leaders point us to where it may have stopped. We form a line to flush it and listen. Our guides are armed with big flashlights to give us a view of it if it flushes. Now we hear it again and begin to run, stumbling in a ragged line toward its call. Running in a marsh is not an act of grace. And I wonder what this sixty-nine-year-old I call myself is doing here careening through the dark, chasing a mouse-like little bird, this...this...this Holy Rail.

Again it escapes our pursuit. Again we hear its call, rush toward it. Silence. Then, with no warning, up it flies, brushing the face of one of the group, and is gone. This time, though, we have seen it—or rather seen a yellowish brown blur in wild flight, more like a great moth than a bird.

Absurd as it may seem, I am happy. And yet I saw or glimpsed the sought-for bird not as well, as clearly, as I would have liked. In fact, I will feel it necessary to explain to people that I didn't have the heart-stirring sensation that goes with a clear, vivid vision of a bird. I will explain that the conditions for seeing were far from perfect, and that I wasn't as quick in my reactions as I might have been. I am, at best, a mediocre watcher, but even mediocre watchers can transcend themselves. I will explain all this. For now I slosh back to the bus, weary but exultant. I have experienced, if only partially, something extraordinary. I have experienced a rare and real presence.

*

It's hard to get to sleep. I'm in a strange place, reliving a strange event. Gradually, as I lie there staring at the moonscape of the ceiling, a resolution forms in my mind. I see that I want to show why it is that a comfort-loving man can find himself running through a night-shrouded marsh far from home, in pursuit of a small bird. And I see also that to put this into words will require more than just offering a few good reasons. For my experience is one of those that defy good reasons and the language of good reasons. I will have to be the complete opportunist, calling upon other voices, upon stories, dreams, inventions. I will have to call upon poetry, the ancient art so useful for expressing the power and meaning of birds in our lives.

I see a book already. It is beautifully bound in royal blue, my name and the title printed in gilt on the spine. I can't make out the title, and from that strange failure I deduce I am sleeping at last and that this is all a dream.

*

I tell two people of the project: my wife and Lewis—can I say this?—my ornithologist.

My wife, no birdwatcher, approves but thinks it somewhat ambitious for a man supposedly enjoying the golden leisure of retirement. "After all," she says, not looking up from her embroidery, "you're only trying to explain the mystery of epiphany." I let her irony glide by, holding only to the lovely word "epiphany," which resonates into the silence that follows. It seems like a term I sought without knowing I sought it.

Lewis also approves but is, as a scientist should be, skeptical of my going at an already elusive subject with no procedure to guide me, no systematic way of acquiring data on which to base a hypothesis, and no apparent means of testing any hypothesis I might come up with. "Why don't you put it in a poem?" he asks. After all these years, I still can't tell when he's serious.

"It won't fit," I reply vaguely.

"Well, it sounds to me like you're turning a nice hobby into a religious experience."

"Some birdwatching *is*, I suppose, a hobby, along with collecting matchbooks and building boats in bottles." My response sounds pettish, even to my own ear. "What I mean is something deeper, more intense, than a hobby."

"Show me!" Lewis says.

*

A poet must be forgiven for going to books first in search of answers. It's a stubborn, inveterate habit. And forgive this poet for going to a poem where a bird is gorgeously celebrated, Hopkins's "The Windhover."

I take the book from the shelf, turn to the poem, note what I should have remembered — that it's dedicated to "Christ our Lord" — and read aloud for the full force of it:

I caught this morning morning's minion, king-
> dom of daylight's dauphin, dapple-dawn-drawn Falcon, in
> his riding
Of the rolling level underneath him steady air, and striding
High there, how he rung upon the rein of a wimpling wing
In his ecstasy! then off, off forth on swing,
> As a skate's heel sweeps smooth on a bow-bend: the hurl
> and gliding
Rebuffed the big wind. My heart in hiding
Stirred for a bird, — the achieve of, the mastery of the thing!

I am brought to a hard stop here, not by the figures and their spectacular gymnastics, not by Hopkins's intention that we should see the bird as an embodiment of supernatural presence and power, but by the simple — so deceptively simple — "My heart in hiding / Stirred for a bird." Is that it? Our hearts hidden only to be brought to light by a bird? I would like to think so. I *do* think so!

I read on, but silently now to the end, close the book and slide it back into its place. It is, after all, a poem for Jesus. I have no license to suit its meaning to my own faith.

Perhaps I need to be out in the field. Perhaps my heart is too good at hiding between the covers of books.

*

The Churchill River meets Hudson Bay at Cape Merry. Both bodies of windy water are brilliant with breaking ice, and I am with my Druidic circle at water's edge. Our platform is a massive gray rock among many massive gray rocks—like a petrified pod of beached whales. We are looking out over the water, birds everywhere: gulls, terns, ducks, geese, jaegers, loons. Suddenly, to the left of us and closer to the water, a man from another group shouts, pointing ahead and to his left, "Snow Bunting!" He knows what I'm looking for. I swing my binoculars around and catch a glimpse of a white flutter, which quickly drops over the edge of a slab of flashing ice.

Now it's a matter of waiting. I don't mind. The air glitters, birds' wings rush overhead, I forget the pain in my lower back, forget everything not connected with being here, a man utterly free of mundane duty. And waiting itself has a relish, for it is not waiting merely, but waiting with the hope of seeing something extraordinary.

*

Epiphany—I want it to mean simply a rare and free showing forth of vital presence. But it's an ancient term and won't be easily stripped of its religious associations; the presence, by its sudden intensity, will seem not just extraordinary but supernatural. Perhaps that's not inappropriate. Birds seem radically different from other creatures.

Donald Culross Peattie tells why:

> Man feels himself an infinity above those creatures who stand, zoölogically, only one step below him, but every human being looks up to the birds.

They seem to us like emissaries of another world which exists about us and above us, but into which, earth-bound, we cannot penetrate. It is not the strength of the lion that we give to angels, but wings.

*

"There! There!" shouts the watcher to our left, alerting me. I try to follow his finger, but he is seeing at a different angle and it takes me—a slow seer—a few seconds to locate the bird. And again what I see is a white blur, heading right and low over the ice, then down and out of sight.

"That's your bunting," he shouts.

I thank him, but without enthusiasm. I've seen it and not seen it. But no one in my group had seen the bunting clearly. When somebody asks if I am going to put the bird on my list, I reply, "On my birds-almost-seen list." On this trip I've spotted with fine clarity a Snowy Owl, a Hawk Owl, a Ross' Gull. But the bird that has my attention is the one I didn't quite see. "Jaegers—Pomarines—overhead!" someone shouts. Still thinking *bunting*, I look up and see the splendid birds, or not birds so much as swift impressions of birds. It may be that intense and full seeing takes more character than I possess.

*

Swift impressions pass easily into dreams, a flurry of white wings, I in hopeless pursuit. Even asleep I could read the crude symbolism and dismissed this dream for another. In it, I possess a gorgeous book, to be handled with the utmost reverence. It contained pictures of birds that would have shamed Audubon, birds that belonged to a higher, sacred order of being. The trouble was that I had misplaced it or lent it out but had forgotten to whom. I scoured my shelves. It was not there, only its fading afterimage as I wake up—this time for good—feeling a sense of profound disappointment.

*

Lewis has given up smoking a pipe but keeps one by him anyway. It is a good pointer when he is explaining something. When he is fishing for a word, he will knock imaginary dottle out of the bowl into an empty ashtray. And when he is impatient, he chews the stem.

He is now chewing the stem.

"Well," he says, "you could have chosen a really rare bird—say the Siberian Rubythroat. Or if you wanted an even snowier Snow Bunting, there's MacKay's. But frankly, Leonard, when you've seen one bunting, you've seen them all."

"Really, Lewis!" I say, shocked at this unscientific indifference to difference. When he smiles with the pipe in his mouth, he seems capable of any mischief.

Before I go, he hands me a book to take with me—Desmond Nethersole-Thompson's *The Snow Bunting*. I already like the book because of the author's name.

*

When I tell my wife how truly shocked I was at Lewis's cynicism, she says, looking up from her embroidery, "This is not all about birds, is it?"

*

"Tweet, tweet." That's the opinion of David, poet, friend, and guest from Philadelphia. By it, he means many things. Among the most obvious: that birdwatching is merely insipid and that by chasing after birds, I had forfeited the seriousness the poet owes the world. David thinks himself tough, unillusioned. For him, the primary obligation of poets is to engage the ugly front of the reality of our time.

"Prettiness," he says, pouring himself his fourth scotch, "is for the birds."

"But David . . ."

"Poems should not be dainty birdhouses," he adds between gulps.

"But David," I say, "that's not fair."

"What's fairness got to do with it?" he says, pouring himself another drink.

I am still nursing my first, wondering whether sobriety put one at a disadvantage in this argument. But I go on, even though it is clear that David is not giving me all his attention.

I point out to him that poetry and birds have been associated from the beginning of civilization, probably before. I remind him that ancient poets put birds into their poems not just as symbols for human feelings but also as authentic forms of otherness. Sappho, when she wants to represent Aphrodite, the Goddess of Love, in her chariot, has it drawn not by horses, the tame servants of humans, but by wild birds, "beautiful swift sparrows" with a whir of "fast-beating wings." Birds appear in poems to show states of mind that go beyond the human. Horace, in one of his odes, imagines himself transformed at his death into a great bird, "the rough skin already" gathering on his legs. This transformation complete, he will soar above the world and death to become a wonder to those gazing up into the heavens from every quarter of the globe. Birds enter poems to mediate between us and the world. There is the poem of the Japanese master, Ōtomo Yakamochi, in which the poet, seeing a lark lift into the brilliant light of a spring sky, feels his heart lift with it.

But most wonderful of all, there is the story of Vālmīki, the great Indian sage.... Here I notice that David is breathing heavily, his chin sunk to his chest.

"David? David!" To hell with David. I will tell my story anyway.

Vālmīki has an ashram near a forest. As is the wont of such men, he regularly purifies himself by bathing in the water of clear streams. On a certain day, the sage—who knows why?—just as he is about to enter such a stream, is taken by the splendor of the forest around him. Instead of stepping into the stream, he walks about awhile and is pleased with what he sees; and more pleased still when his eyes fall on "an inseparable pair of sweet-voiced *Krauncha* birds." But even as he is enjoying the loving gestures of their courtship, the male is struck down by the arrow of a malicious *Nishāda,* or low-caste hunter. When the male falls dead, his mate cries out piteously and Vālmīki, deeply moved, utters a terrible curse on the hunter.

And so the story goes—so far unremarkable. And yet not quite unremarkable. Something has shut all else out of Vālmīki's awareness. But what? What has so shaken the usually imperturbable sage? It is the curse—no ordinary curse, but one that has burst out of him in the form of a well-turned couplet! The sage is astounded. He has, it seems, just invented poetry. Invented something new out of very old materials: compassion, rage, and grief. From this raw stuff he has created a beautifully ordered thought, and from loss created its own consolation.

No one has done such a thing before. Which is to say that Vālmīki is the first, the father, of all poets. He is also the first known birdwatcher, and it is his birdwatching that has occasioned his invention: from *shoka* (grief) comes *shloka* (poetry).

It may be something of an anticlimax to find that the god Brahma has put the first poem in Vālmīki's head to prepare the sage for composing the epic *Rāmāyana*, the life and deeds of the divine hero, Rāma. The episode in the forest having served its purpose, the epic can now begin. And does, very slowly unfolding over thousands of lines.

But I am still in the forest, held there by Vālmīki's wonder and outrage, and by his joy in making poetry of these human passions. And perhaps there is a subtler sense in all this: It's as though, before the sage can imagine divine and deep doings, he must see and feel what the world offers its denizens—desolation of death, sweetness of love. For Vālmīki, as for Wordsworth, this world, after all,

> ...is the world
> Of all of us,—the place where, in the end,
> We find our happiness, or not at all!

*

Next morning, David, with a surly nod at his host, sits down at the kitchen table, reaches for his coffee, and notes as he does so a book opened by his cup. He pauses in mid-gesture and reads:

The Bird Watcher
BY CARL DENNIS

Now the coast of the country is grazed by light.
Farmers are rising in America.
Hunters in the North shoulder their guns
And march off into the woods.
The sky is crowded with small birds.
Unnoticed they scatter across fields and towns.

Now in the twilight before work
In his one moment of leisure
The bird watcher steps out of his house
To stand in the street and wait.

If a single stray circles nearby
Or calls from a maze of branches,
Or hovers as a speck far off,
The watcher, with no one nearby to look,
Points up, and with no one to listen
Breaks the silence, sounding out the name.

He looks up at me, and lifts his cup as in a toast. Nothing more is said about birds.

*

A male Hooded Warbler was reported seen in the park seven minutes from my house. I am out there in six, but a half dozen others have arrived ahead of me. It's 9:30, a cool, clear spring morning. First-rate for seeing birds. We take the trail where the warbler was last spotted. Up the hill and into the oak woods, then down and into pines, then willows. There the trail ends. No bird. The others decide to take the same trail back; I go solo down the parallel lower trail. They say they'll shout if they see the warbler. Ten minutes later I hear shouting. Could it be? It could be. But I'm halfway down now, and it would take me some minutes to run back and up the other trail. And suppose it was someone else, shouting for something other than birds? I go on, come out at the end and meet them, who, of course, have seen the bird. They go, and I stay to wander the trails till noon, then give up and go home.

Next morning I am out again but earlier, take the upper trail and find nothing. Do I hear a fragment of song? Perhaps from the lower trail. I studied pictures of the bird last night. A little beauty—black hood, bright yellow face and undersides, lovely and complex song.

I don't hesitate—down the lower trail. I take no more than fifteen steps, look up and see it perched a little above eye level in a willow to the left of the trail and not more than ten feet ahead. It begins to sing, and I would like to sing with it, but instead address it with terms of endearment and do a restrained two-step shuffle. There it is, *Wilsonia citrina*—is it really lemon colored? I see it and see it. There is a wonderful convergence here—of its freedom and my purpose. This is epiphany or nothing is. I am a happy—no, an ecstatic man. Even when it flies. As it now does and with my best wishes.

*

When I tell Lewis all this, he shrugs: "You know, you may merely have experienced the hunter's joy at capturing and subduing his prey—not quite epiphany, I believe."

"But I'm *not* a hunter. I wasn't trying to capture or subdue." My voice rises in denial. "All I wanted was to see as wholly as I could."

"Perhaps it only seems that way because civilization has domesticated hunting to the point that the desire to capture and subdue is disguised as passive observation. What you do is so refined that the old passion for the blood hunt has been attenuated into gazing through several layers of lens." Lewis thrusts his pipe into the air. I'm about to get a lecture.

"Lewis...," I say.

"No. No. Listen, you ought to know your origins. The tradition of your genteel pastime goes back to the eighteenth century—the great age of the amateur—when leisured members of the educated middle class began collecting bird lore, partly as a contribution to scientific knowledge but mostly for the fun of it—a hobby, I'm afraid. And behind this hobby lay an older tradition that lives on into our century: birding—collecting birds, dead or alive, for food, for plumage, for pets, for study."

"That's precisely why I resist the term 'birding,'" I say.

"Well, you can resist all you want but you're going to lose on that one. Birdwatching these days sounds a little quaint, a silly old-fashioned pastime of English eccentrics. And besides, the word 'birding' has some zip to it, some active purpose. When I think of birdwatching, I see comfortable elders lollygagging over a little wildflower just off the trail, or stooping to pick up an odd seashell."

"But birding," I say, "according to Peterson anyway, tends to be associated with list making, with identification."

"Well, yes, the old hunting impulse at work there—the list is a substitute for the kill."

"I don't think, in any case, that birding as you define it has much to do with what I'm talking about. Just the opposite. It reduces the real presence of a bird to a name and number."

"If you exclude birders from your religion," here Lewis points his pipestem at me, like a gun barrel, "you'll have to exclude along with them lots of others: for instance, people who just want to get away from it all, and who find birds nice enough but no reason to change their church affiliation. And those to whom interest in birds is just a part of an interest in all nature. All these you're going to deny the privilege of your epiphany? That leaves the poets and likeminded sensitive souls. A rather exclusive club, I'd say!"

Here a silence ensues. I believe Lewis is wrong but have no good answer to his question and now he asks another one, "By the by, how do you *tell* when you've had one of these epiphanies?"

＊

Browsing again among my books, I find support—but for Lewis, and from the most unlikely places. This from John Ruskin:

> The heads of birds of prey are always beautiful, and used as the richest ornaments in all ages.

And this from Havelock Ellis:

> Of birds the knowledge of poets generally is of the most generalised and elementary kind; they are the laughing-stock of the ornithologist; they are only a stage removed from the standpoint of the painter who was introducing a tree into his landscape and when asked what tree, replied, 'Oh, just the ordinary tree.' Even Goethe mistook the finches by the roadside for larks.

But Goethe, in conversation with Eckermann, strikes back for the both of us:

> The ornithologists...are probably delighted when they have brought any peculiar bird under some head; still, Nature carries on her own free sport, without troubling herself with the classes marked out by limited men.

*

I open Peterson's *Field Guide to Western Birds* to the Snow Bunting, Family *Emberizidae*, Genus *Plectrophenax*, Species *nivalis*. Dead languages to name a living bird. Odder yet, the bird is accused of falsehood in its generic name, which signifies impostor or cheat for its false-seeming longspur-like rear toe. Neither is its plumage all white. Like its bill, much of its upper part is black. But in spring when, as Peterson puts it, Snow Buntings "often swirl over snowy fields in large flocks," they seem all white. It's then that they live up to another name for them, Snow Flake.

They breed far north, have been observed, according to Nethersole-Thompson, near the North Pole, but winter as far south (although rarely) as northern California.

But they are not so wholly white as MacKay's Bunting and have, like other less striking birds, their share of trials to bear: blow-fly maggots, hen fleas, feather lice, worms. Nethersole-Thompson, who provides us with this information, loves and admires the little bird, and for no very good scientific reason: it is beautiful and brave, "possibly the most romantic and elusive bird in the British Isles, and almost certainly the hardiest small bird in the world." Only the lucky "may see the cock snow bird's remarkable display flight and listen to a song which is full of wildness and desire."

But words are abstract and general, pictures flatly two-dimensional. In the absence of the real bird, these merely

whet my wish for the real thing. And make its absence the
more intense. Writes Walter Pavlich:

> Field guides explain color,
> vagrant range,
>
> the vague translations of a song,
> but nothing of the distance
> that develops into absence.

*

"OK," Lewis says. "Suppose we grant you your epiphany,
this experience of intense presence, how about the second
experience, the third, the fifty-third? If the experience
fades out, however gradually, isn't what you've been calling
epiphany simply novelty, the psychological charge in seeing a new and perhaps handsome bird? When you've seen
Plectrophenax nivalis a dozen times, you may just yawn or
chase after a new thrill.

"Did you know that Virginia Woolf, when she was
having psychological troubles, heard the birds singing in
Greek? I just read that somewhere."

"Yes, Lewis, I knew it."

"Remarkable. I gather she knew Greek. I wonder what
they sang about."

*

I want support against Lewis's skepticism. But there is, so far as I'm aware, no *Philosophy of Birding* or *Apologia for Birdwatching*. So I have to sift and sift. But one must be wary. Apparent friends can prove unwitting enemies. Take this from John Burroughs:

> The very idea of a bird is a symbol and a suggestion to the poet. A bird seems to be at the top of the scale, so vehement and intense is his life—large brained, large lunged, hot, ecstatic, his frame charged with buoyancy and his heart with song. The beautiful vagabonds, endowed with every grace, masters of all climes, and knowing no bounds,—how many human aspirations are realized in their free, holiday-lives—and how many suggestions to the poet in their flight and song!

This with its gorgeous eloquence generates some of the excitement birdwatchers in general, not just poets, can feel. But such eloquence exacts its price, a sentimentality that overstates the case, or falsifies it: "beautiful vagabonds," "free, holiday-lives." Ask the Red-tailed Hawk about free holiday-lives as it stoops on its prey, or ask the Scrub Jay in its talons as it rises again. Burroughs seems to be thinking of those sweet-singing larks and thrushes that so comfortably inhabit poems, not the matter-of-fact birds unnoticed outside his window.

I want matter-of-fact ones in my proofs, the kind Dar-

win referred to when he cautioned us not to anthropomor-
phize birds:

> We behold the face of nature bright with glad-
> ness, we often see superabundance of food; we do
> not see, or we forget, that the birds which are idly
> singing round us mostly live on insects or seeds,
> and are thus constantly destroying life; or we for-
> get how largely these songsters, or their eggs, or
> their nestlings, are destroyed by birds and beasts
> of prey; . . .

*

Lewis says, "A series of apt quotes does not constitute an
argument. Show me."

*

Naomi phones. The group is going out to the Old Ranch.
Not much around in late summer, but the Rare Bird Alert
reports a Black-and-white Warbler there. The group—
Thursday's Children—consists of a core of four or five
regulars and five or six members more loosely connected.
We go out birdwatching almost every Thursday, pooling
cars, heading where opportunity calls.

We have no official leader, but Naomi, the oldest among
us, is our unofficial one. She is in her early seventies and
shows no signs of slowing down. Out in the field her only

concession to age is her three-legged folding stool slung over one shoulder, along with her binoculars and spotting scope. A few months back she underwent major surgery. Moreover, she has probably seen this bird a thousand times in her forty years of birdwatching, and seen it when her eyes were far sharper, her hearing able to catch the highest notes the bird can sing. Yet here she is, as intent on finding the least movement in the leaves as if she had never seen this particular warbler before.

In some sense she hasn't. We can never quite exhaust presence. It's too dynamic, and it shows us, like the moon, only one side at a time. A principle of indeterminacy rules in birdwatching as well as in particle physics: The more we concentrate on the whole, the more we miss the detail; the more we concentrate on the detail, the more we miss the whole. There is no help for it.

When I ask Naomi if her many sightings of the warbler might dull this one, or if she gets the same thrill out of the experience, she thinks awhile, then says, "No, it's not quite the same. I'm anyway pretty old for thrills."

Just then something flutters high in the cypress in front of us. All binoculars go up, hers as quickly as anyone's. False alarm—White-crowned Sparrow, a junk bird at this time of year. Naomi, I believe, understates her response, perhaps out of the tact that many birdwatchers develop. No doubt the experience of first sight is more intense, but, if watchers have passion enough to keep on seriously looking, the thousandth spotting has something for them still.

Hearts, even old ones, quicken at the right summons. I'm sure of that.

But who's to say what's in the heart of Dan, the tall, bearded young man—thirty-five or so—standing beside Naomi. He is still sweeping the foliage for a bird that's no stranger to his quick eyes. He has seen it on the Pacific slopes of Costa Rica, at Laguna Atascosa on the Texas Gulf Coast, and again at Cape May, and yet again at San Francisco's Golden Gate Park, and so on and on. But here he is out for another look. And at an hour of the day when those of his age are thinking about a break at the water cooler or are beginning to count the hours before lunch. How does he do it? He does it in spasms. He holds a job just long enough to support these intense stretches of watching, then back to work. Any job will do. Mostly, one suspects, the jobs are those that pay just enough for the economy class in all departments of his life. For him such work must be at best a paying avocation. No one observing him in the field for an hour could mistake his true vocation.

He cannot afford the expensive gear that many of his fellow watchers carry. He has no scope, only a much-scuffed, smallish pair of binoculars, which he carries in one hand. The rest of his equipment is what nature gave and he has cultivated. Perhaps he even considers his disadvantages—if that's what they are—as spice to enliven his watching, which is obviously a very serious matter.

I met Dan once by chance in fields far south of where

we now stand. He was looking up, identifying birds aloud—there were many, seeming to come from all directions. As he ticked off names, he miscalled one and was corrected by a professional guide. Some time had passed between that meeting and our next, but the first thing he did was explain to me, to whom he owed no explanation, why he had erred. A very serious matter.

But I here confess a reservation about Dan—that perhaps he is more birder than birdwatcher, that he is more hunter than looker-on, more passionate about having seen than seeing. But I'm not sure. He's one of our peripheral group and from time to time is off on his own or with another man about his age. We meet them out in the field now and then, and he has such a look in his eye—a relentless sort of glitter.

Maybe there's more than one kind of epiphany.

*

In the glove compartment of my car is a postcard from an East Coast friend, who keeps in touch solely by this means. On this card, a quote (with no comment) from the *Shvetāshvatara Upanishad*, one of the ancient Hindu scriptures:

> Two birds, really one and known by the same name, sit in the same tree. One eats the tree's sweet fruit while the other watches.

I thought the quote would amuse Thursday's Children, but decide now that it isn't meant to be amusing. On the picture side of the card is a caged pair of pale blue lovebirds, one feeding the other.

*

We have not seen our warbler. Either it has flown off or was misreported. In any case, the nine of us are straggling back to the road where we left our cars. We are not overly disappointed. This bird was nowhere near a first for any of us. Still, it would have been good to see. We discuss other possibilities—the lighthouse perhaps. Or the Willows. We just about reach the road when a van pulls up, two men in the front seats. They have the avid look of birders. We wave, and the man on the passenger side rolls down his window and shouts, "A Snow Bunting! Across from the turnoff to South Beach!" and off they roar. We look at each other. A Snow Bunting! That's news to lift the heart.

Some of us have seen it before, but long ago; others have glimpsed it; a few have missed it altogether. Everyone wants a look, but I wonder if the bird has the same meaning for them as it does for me. I note that we climb in the three cars with more than ordinary haste and are moving out with more than ordinary speed.

But why am I rushing? It is after all a flesh-and-blood bird, no more or less so than the blackbirds we pass in their hundreds at the dairy farm. Why am I rushing? My back and neck still ache from watching for the warbler, and here I am no doubt hurrying toward another occasion for regret. I smile at my folly but keep my speed where it is, in fact accelerate a bit, bringing me too near the car in front of me, the car in which Naomi hunches over the wheel, herself a little too close to Dan's car ahead of her. We are a parade of purposefulness, pursuers of a vision. My three passengers are uncharacteristically quiet. Only Claire speaks—"Wouldn't *that* be something!"—and then subsides into silence. A boy on the side of the road, after we have passed him, lifts his hand in a tentative wave. I catch him in my mirror and lift my hand, even though he won't see it.

And I am not a hunter!

*

Lewis once told me a story about Frank Pitelka, a famous colleague of his, who, when he was a young man, was asked to accompany some important fellow in pursuit of birds out into cold Arctic fields. As a conscientious guide, Pitelka was pointing out various species, among them a flock of Common Eiders. When he looked harder at these, he saw that one of the birds was a much rarer Spectacled Eider and turned to tell his companion, who never looked up, so busy was he writing down all that he had "seen."

*

We pull over on the weedy margin between the macadam and a barbed-wire fence, our three cars parking by four others and a van already there. Fifteen people with binoculars in hand are standing in a semicircle, facing out on the burnt gold of the slope where the bird was supposed to be. I recognize the two who passed the news on to us, and a half dozen others are familiar to me. It is clear that there is no Snow Bunting around. If there were, they wouldn't be quietly chatting. Slowly we get out of our cars and join them. The air, as though at peace with itself, is calm. There is a sweetness in this calm, and a melancholy too.

It reminds me of George Tooker's painting called *Bird Watchers* that depicts a group of people rather formally dressed, in what seems to be a city park. Some carry binoculars, some don't. Birds are around them but they don't seem to see them. A man, who might be their leader, his arms hanging at his sides, shows us his empty palms—a listless gesture of futility or puzzlement. All the faces are serenely waiting—for what? Serene and sad, like the subdued winter colors of their world.

*

Lewis is on a field trip. I write him a note: "(1) Epiphany can happen to anyone capable of receiving. (2) You *know* you have an epiphany when you experience the shock of recognition. I hope this answers your questions."

Lewis replies in his tiny, beautifully clear hand: "Shock of recognition?"

And I back: "'Shock of recognition,' borrowed by Edmund Wilson from Herman Melville. Wilson meant meeting of good writer with bad one. Melville meant meeting of genius with genius (Melville meets Hawthorne?). I mean the electric experience when epiphany occurs, when hope or surprise meets intense presence. Why are watchers reluctant to lower their binoculars? To make sure of the identity of the bird, yes, but also from a strong desire to prolong so special a seeing, not the consummation of the hunt, but the experience of knowledge. The meaning and mystery of otherness."

Lewis's prodding reply after: "Knowledge?"

My answer: "Not, Lewis, knowledge of the bird as an ornithological specimen—a collection of biological mechanisms. But knowledge of a meaning, only intuitively grasped, of the wholeness of being, in this case, of bird being."

"Why 'shock'?"

My answer: "Shock because we live insulated by habit, convention, ideas—all devices by which we shelter ourselves from dangerously direct contact with actuality. Direct contact is what shocks us. But we dearly need such shocks to keep ourselves engaged in our real circumstances, which, if full of peril, are also full of life-giving wonder and beauty. How's that?"

From Lewis: "Mmmmm. Rather mystical, don't you think?"

Me again, out of pique:

> there is throughout nature something mocking, something that leads us on and on, but arrives nowhere; keeps no faith with us. All promise outruns the performance. We live in a system of approximations. Every end is prospective of some other end, which is also temporary; a round and final success nowhere. We are encamped in nature, not domesticated.... Our music, our poetry, our language itself are not satisfactions, but suggestions.

I mean to shake him up a little with this specimen from Emerson, but manage also to do the same to myself. But I think Ralph Waldo is more on my side than on Lewis's. And I'm glad to have him there.

*

No one knows how the Snow Bunting rumor got started. It seems to have congealed out of the air. Why should birdwatchers be less susceptible to illusory hope than other groups when our interest—passion—is at stake?

So we climb slowly into our cars and drive off, our group heading home. Just as I start speeding up, a Whitecrowned Sparrow darts past the windshield. This event too is a shock. To someone somewhere, this modest little creature is a rare bird.

*

I dream of the sacred book of birds again. I dream that I open it to an account of a fifteenth-century Italian traveler, one Virgilio Stampari, concerning the poet Abu Ibn Sulam, who, blind from birth, is reputed to have composed 999 poems, each with a different bird in it, some of them — like the Silver Sparrow and the Rainbow Cuckoo — already extinct before the Flood. Not a single example of Abu's work remains. For to this poet, to sing was to compose — or to compose was to sing. Thus his poems flew off into the air like birds loosed from a cage.

Stampari also tells us that crouched at the poet's knee was a slave boy who could whistle to perfection the song of any bird that came to drink or bathe in the waters of the fountain on whose steps the poet sat every day, all day. The boy was otherwise mute, his tongue cut out by the pirates who sold him to the poet. Listening to the boy's imitation of a song, Abu would promptly create from it a poetic bird more vivid, more alive, more whole than the original.

Stampari was not an eyewitness to this marvel but, he tells us, offers the reports of Syrian merchants, how trustworthy he neglects to say. He concludes with this cryptic observation: "Perhaps after all, truth follows fact, although at some distance, but the mouth is a cunning instrument."

*

Lewis, his pipe at the ready, comes at me from a new angle: "Say that you are out with a group of fellow watchers. You are walking somewhat ahead of the group, which is strung out on a path through a marshy area. Suddenly you see a duck out on one of the little pools in the reeds. You can see with your naked eye it's no ordinary duck. Up fly your binoculars. It takes you a few seconds but then you whisper the name, 'Shelduck!' And you beckon the people behind you and shout softly, 'Shelduck!' This is happiness—a combination of surprise and delight. This is good stuff.

"Or seems to be. The group hurries up, among them your leader. She takes one rather perfunctory glance, shrugs, and shakes her head: 'Sorry. Not for the list, unless you keep a list of escapees. This is from some zoo or private aviary.'

"Now suppose you give up listing the bird, or list it with a proviso that, according to the (strange) rules of this activity, it can't really be counted. Suppose all this; what then do you do with the epiphany you think you had on seeing the duck? Have you all this time been deluded about the nature of such experiences? Have you worshiped false idols and paid the price? Have you simply asked too much meaning from nature or from your feelings?

"It's true that if you know a bird to be a captive, see it behind a wire fence, your reaction to it will be conditioned, even compromised, by that knowledge. But here is an instance where you believed with your whole heart and soul that this was one of nature's free and untrammeled creatures. And what do you find?—a cheating anomaly. Where you have every right to expect a rare but nevertheless natural effect stemming from a natural cause, some greedy, careless, or indifferent hand has intervened and soiled the process of recognition. What now? Where is your epiphany? And your shock of recognition, a phrase that now, I believe, takes on an altogether new meaning under these circumstances?"

I race through my mind—no help there—and pull up a lame, "How often does a thing like this occur?"

Lewis waves a finger at me. "If it happened only once, you would still be obliged to answer for it."

Of course, he's right. So I try, hesitantly, to construct a decent response: "All I would want, Lewis, is to save the epiphany. First, I would have *had* it—and in what sense would *that* experience be false? Good effects can come of bad or tainted causes. My frame of mind when I spotted the shelduck would grant the bird its freedom to be where and what it was on its own account. If this freedom were based on a false premise, were—well—ambiguous, nevertheless the experience of seeing in itself would still be unaltered by that. Whatever came after wouldn't touch the integrity of the epiphany."

Lewis waves all this aside, and, rising to go, says, "On this principle you could build a whole world based on an initial error or misperception, a whole delusory world."

After he is out the door, I say to him, "What else is the story of Adam and Eve?"

*

As I am drifting into sleep, a question flashes over my fading consciousness, a question worthy of Lewis: If only the naive or ignorant can experience the out-of-place shelduck, does it follow that the more one knows, the less one is apt to experience epiphany? Is there a hidden cost here?

I have a flawless answer but mislay it in sleep.

*

Heading out to the lighthouse one misty morning, I see a man standing in a newly plowed field at Far Corners—a solitary figure, a gawky elder fooling with his scope on the soft, dark, broken soil. But there are two cars pulled off the road, one apparently his, the other belonging to the gray-haired woman now walking toward the gate to the field.

I pull over, I'm not sure why, to watch those two. They are all brown or gray as of a time before color. There is something grainy and rough-edged about them, like characters from a poem by Thomas Hardy, where lives, otherwise homely, often have the beauty of tough coherence and solemn direction.

This, of course, is from far-off. Up closer perhaps it would all seem different. I make up my mind to give them a poem someday.

*

My wife finds a dead thrush on our back porch, its neck broken when it flew into the plate-glass window. A Hermit Thrush. Then later another, also with a broken neck. Held in the hand they are small and soft, nothing like their sturdy pictured selves in the books. I remember many years back finding a robin, still alive, fallen in a patch of violets in our yard. My son, then five, was fascinated; in my ignorance, I promised to see if I could save the bird. I picked it up and felt it twitch a few times in my palm, then it died, stiffening already as I set it back down. Father and son looked at each other for what seemed a very long time. Father then made some banal remark about picking up strange things, went into the house, into the bathroom, and washed and washed his hands.

There are probably many kinds of epiphany.

*

The poet Coleridge, obsessed all his life by strangeness, often enough experienced shocks of recognition. They are recorded in his poetry. But on one occasion, he chose to put such an experience into prose, a prose that reads like some haunted passage out of Edgar Allan Poe.

> Once, when our path was over-canopied by the meeting boughs, as I halloed to those a stone-throw behind me, a sudden flash of light dashed down, as it were, upon the path close before me,

> with such rapid and indescribable effect that my
> life seemed snatched away from me—not by ter-
> ror but by the whole attention being suddenly
> and unexpectedly seized hold of—if one could
> conceive a violent blow given by an unseen hand,
> yet without pain or local sense of injury, of the
> weight falling here or there, it might assist in con-
> ceiving the feeling. This I found was occasioned
> by some very large bird, who, scared by my noise,
> had suddenly flown upward, and by the spring of
> his feet or body had driven down the branch on
> which he was aperch.

The shock of recognition here is not joyous. Nor is it fearful. But it leaves behind a sense of oppression, heaviness. It's as though the poet had walked by accident into another world, like his own in every respect but somehow dangerously different. I notice he does not give a specific name to the bird or tree. But Coleridge knew the names of birds and trees in his world.

And he must have known something else: Not all presence is open to interpretation. It takes considerable tact to pass on, to leave things inscrutably be.

*

Morning. I am in my study, a cup of coffee at my elbow. I am not entirely awake yet. Without thinking, I turn a page and my eye falls on a geologic timetable stretching back one hundred fifty million years, and I find myself instinctively narrowing my concentration. I choose one epoch in all that ungraspable expanse—the Jurassic, because I know there I will find this phrase: "The first birds (*Archaeopteryx*)." Hungering for something concrete to grip in the empty reaches of millennial abstraction, I try to see beyond, or past, words, but all that comes flapping up is the Disney image of a pterodactyl, a bony, black silhouette against a dull red sky, slowly, laboriously creaking past in the mindless solitudes of pure extension. And this melancholy figure begins to dissolve like smoke even before it crosses the outer edge of my sleepy, nearsighted attention.

Out the window, meanwhile, a California Towhee feeds complacently in the shade of the black pine. I stare at it as a man would who saw something incredible, although I have no doubt of its presence and its identity. It's just that for the moment I can't put things together: distance with proximity; time past (or time that never was) with time present; the strange, the wildly strange, with the familiar; otherness with my mind; and even my own mind with itself. I am giddy, I am momentarily someone not of this place or time, not what I seem, a strange creature like a secret agent on a mission he has somehow forgotten.

But this too passes.

*

Thursday's Children, out all morning, are heading for lunch. I am in Ursula's car. Ursula is a tall, handsome Norwegian woman of about forty, who, although she took up birdwatching late, is very good at it. However, she is apt to wander off to look at wildflowers when others are in hot pursuit of a bird. She has just braked and reversed so that we can all see the Western Bluebird perched on the top wire of the fence that runs by the road. We are making the proper sounds of pleasure when, in the backseat, Naomi and Claire get into an argument. Claire likes to argue, but not for long. If you don't agree with her first point, she is apt to give up on you. The issue: Why do bluebirds, hardly rare, elicit our wonder and admiration? Ah, I think, this is epiphany talk.

"The color blue," Claire says, "is charismatic."

"As in Scrub Jays," Naomi says dryly.

"That's different."

"How different?"

"You know."

"Do I?"

"Yes."

And, oddly, that seems to settle the issue. Or to leave it peaceably unsettled.

Later, when they drop me off home, I go rummaging through my books in search of a key to the mysterious attraction of bluebirds, their power to become epiphany even for those who are not birdwatchers. I find nothing, or only this to confirm the effect without explaining the cause:

Ludlow Griscom, in a description of the bird, says, "Common and beloved in the East, local in the far West." We can supplement this enigmatic, curiously unsymmetrical remark with the observation that they are also beloved in the West, although we don't know why. Scrub Jays—more brilliant blue in spring plumage but with the bad manners of their genus—remain to most of us brutish and nasty.

But why shouldn't any bird under the right circumstances become epiphany? Why shouldn't a jay, a White-crowned Sparrow, a blackbird become the intense immediate presence that elicits a sense of profound wonder and of an equally profound, if inexpressible, sense of meaning? Why couldn't a starling, a raven?

I believe that I have just asked what is called a rhetorical question. The anthropologist Loren Eiseley, in a day buried under fog, all but collides with a crow, utterly lost in the dense gray. Both are shocked. Both are aware something eerie has happened that, in some subtle way, changes their lives, even if only to leave behind a small, indissoluble deposit of wonder: "He and I share a viewpoint in common: our worlds have interpenetrated, and we both have faith in the miraculous."

*

Another six words from my postcard friend: "Have you thought of Saint Francis?"

I haven't. I reply, also in six words: "No. Thanks for the little flower."

*

A few years ago, my wife and I visited Assisi and, having arrived early, had the Basilica almost all to ourselves. But much as the murals moved me, I don't remember finding in them the childlike beggar in tatters, the simple saint of folklore. But I may not have been seeing well for having to see so much.

Nevertheless, as we stepped into the sunlight and saw the tour buses, one after another, roll into the parking lot below, we were grateful to have been granted the quiet look the paintings deserve. It might take a different sort of Francis to preach to buses.

I find now, in a battered paperback, that it is not the Francis of *The Little Flowers* preaching to the birds who moves me—although there is that lovely aside in which he hushes the swallows that were distracting him with their singing like children chattering in church. This preacher to the birds tells them that they must be grateful to God for all the blessings He has showered on them. Fair enough, but maybe a little patronizing.

It's the Francis of *Considerations on the Stigmata* who touches me, the footsore traveler who, resting under an oak at the foot of Mount Alverna, takes a moment to study the natural wonders around him. And, as he gazes out over the valley below, birds in their thousands and of all kinds suddenly fly in and circle him, singing and fluttering their wings in evident delight. It appears that they only want to be near him. They settle on his head, shoulders, arms, lap, even around his feet. He sits entirely still, not wishing to disturb them, for he wants to be near them too—so much life, so much beauty, so much joy.

His companions are amazed. Francis, smiling, says to them, "I believe, my dearest brothers, that it pleases our Lord Jesus Christ that we live on this solitary mountain, since our sisters and brothers the birds show such happiness at our coming."

No doubt about it. He has had an epiphany, and an epiphany of such magnitude that only a saint, only one with a boundless capacity for epiphanies, could fully recognize it.

Where there is real presence, there we should put down our burden and abide.

*

A bright, sunshiny spring day, almost too bright. Ursula, her binoculars up to scan a far-off mound of blackberry bushes, asks me, out of nowhere and more in a tone of command than of question, "You're doing a book of bird stories!"

"Um, not exactly," I answer. Ursula doesn't often ask personal questions, so I feel the need to be careful. "It's a sort of . . . well . . . meditation on birdwatching. And . . ."

A little yelp cuts me off. "Wait!" she cries. "Wait! I think we've got our chat. Lefthand top of the biggest bush at eleven o'clock." Naomi, who has been hearing the chat since we arrived, seconds the opinion, and Claire turns to me to ask if I've got it.

"Yes," I say, slow as usual. And unsatisfied. It is a good two hundred yards out in the fenced field, perched in the bright glare, which turns it gray to the naked eye. Binoculars bring in its yellow breast and a hint of its white spectacles. I doubt that, without the testimony of the group, I could be sure of it.

Ursula has set up her powerful scope and invites us to view the bird through it. When it comes my turn, I can see the bird better, but still it's sun dimmed. It's a first for me, but I make no noise about this fact because it is not—what?—real enough, this smoky similitude of the actual thing. Part of epiphany is its sudden, luminous clarity.

As often happens to me out in the field (one reason I will never be a good watcher), my mind drifts with the momentum of reverie. I feel a little isolated knowing that my companions share in their confidence about the identity of the chat. But I feel grateful too—for their generosity in trying to share their confidence with me. And suddenly it seems to me that I have understated that generosity in my effort to concentrate on the personal quality of epiphany. Very few watchers are ungenerous in sharing their seeing. Perhaps those in fanatic pursuit of a new bird for their lists are the exception. But the others are almost always ready to guide the eyes that still cannot see to the bird: "Stand here. That's it. Directly in front of me, and look just a little to the left of the trunk about eye level. That's right. Got it? Good!" Or they are ready to step aside and let those behind pass to the front on a narrow path. I speak with the authority of one who has benefited from such occasions.

As I swim through this milky gratitude, my mind faraway from where I now stand, I remember that I was about to finish my answer to Ursula when the chat seized our attention. In my present slightly sentimental mood, I am about to open my mouth to this purpose when Claire and Naomi, both of whom had walked some distance on, signal us to come to where they stand. They have spotted a Blue Grosbeak on another berry bush, the natural radiance of its plumage subdued to a dingy gray. I am glad to have seen it before in its full brilliance.

"Here, take a look through the scope. Everybody see it?" Two Barn Swallows whip by, their shadows rippling over us. Now I realize the obvious: Ursula wants no more answer. She is out here for birds, not explanations. And so should I be.

*

"Ursula," I say long after she has gone her way, "I mean birds don't *have* stories. That's—almost—the point. That they don't have stories should be for us one of their most prized attributes. Seeing them, we now and then get a glimpse of another world whose denizens do not drag the long chains of cause and effect. When birds fly, they fly always now, untrammeled by regrets for the past, hopes for the future. Winged being. 'Many birds,' so says the philosopher Kant, are 'self-subsisting beauties which are not appurtenant to any object defined with respect to its end, but please freely and on their own account.' How should such creatures have stories to tie them to mere time and space?

"I have heard it argued that there is no such thing as natural history, since we can never get at the motives of nonhuman organisms, let alone rocks and water. I suppose this issue is a matter of definition—of what we think nature is, history is. But surely it can be said without arousing the scorn of natural scientists, even ornithologists, that birds *among themselves have no history*. They live solely and wholeheartedly in the present, and to get to know what they are, not how they have become what they are, one must sometimes live with them in the present, solely and wholeheartedly.

"That's why, Ursula, you were right to cut me short this afternoon. As if you didn't know."

*

It is told that when an old rabbi offered to teach Rabbi Shneur Zalman of Ladi the language of birds and plants, the latter refused, remarking that there was but "*one* thing men need understand." Later, an old man himself, Rabbi Zalman pointed out to his grandson, as they rode through the countryside, that birds were busy everywhere. Sticking his head out the carriage window, he added, "How fast they chatter. . . . They have their own alphabet. All you need do is listen and grasp well, and you will understand their language."

*

I read my five-year-old grandson passages from Poe's "The Raven." A silly spooky poem with which I hope to stir his interest in birds and poetry. When I point to a real raven flying over, he lowers his voice and intones, "Nevermore." We are amused. But I am also worried. I can look over his head into the future, not very far, but far enough to see a smoky sky emptied of birds, who will only live on in books. We will have the names, but the names will no longer summon up actual birds, only pictures of them, virtual reality that will superimpose one more layer between us and our lives. I blink, shake my head, lower my voice and intone, "Nevermore." We laugh and go on.

*

A clerk in a bookstore, watching me write out a check for a new field guide, asks me if being left-handed handicapped my birdwatching. I look up and say, "Not till now."

*

Lewis suddenly smiles. And when I ask why, he says, "It just occurred to me that your pursuit of the bunting repeats an American archetypal fable."

"What," I ask warily, "would that be?"

"Ahab's quest for the white whale. Your bunting is a pint-sized Moby-Dick. And we know how *that* story ends."

*

My wife has brought me a present—for no particular occasion, just a fond gesture. A thick book called *Birds in Our Lives*, published by the U.S. Department of the Interior, edited by Alfred Stefferud, a name new to me. It has a strongly ecological slant (Stewart L. Udall, then Secretary of the Interior, writes its preface) but covers a wide range of bird-related topics, from birds in the Bible to birds and laws that protect them. The date of publication is 1966, the Johnson administration, not so long ago for anyone over forty. But when I begin browsing through it, it seems to belong to another age, an age of black, white, and gray—no color in its photographs and drawings. The birds, and not just the birds, belong to a world of pastness, and I think the odor they would give off, if we could catch it, would be the comfortable mustiness of secondhand bookstores.

There is about the whole book the pathos of old movies. The next-to-last photograph is of a group of people looking at the ducks from over a fence at Lake Merritt in Oakland, California. Two women are carrying babies, a third is feeding the ducks, while her husband holds another baby. An elderly man, cigarette in hand, gazes past the birds. A park attendant (inside the fence) looks calmly on. In the twenty-eight years that have passed since that moment, everything has changed for that small group, and generations of ducks have come and gone. And I myself have stood in that same place more than once, a man different from the man who writes this now. And yet the same.

*

Birdwatching has no bible, but sometimes I open some book at seeming random (or in search of something else) and find exactly what I should have been looking for, this time a passage from W. H. Hudson's *Birds and Man*:

> We are not like children gathering painted shells and pebbles on a beach; but, whether we know it or not, are seeking after something beyond and above knowledge. The wilderness in which we are sojourners is not our home; it is enough that its herbs and roots and wild fruits nourish and give us strength to go onward. Intellectual curiosity, with the gratification of the individual for its only purpose, has no place in this scheme of things as we conceive it. Heart and soul are with the brain in all investigation—a truth which some know in rare, beautiful intervals, and others never; but we are all meanwhile busy with our

> work, like myriads of social insects engaged in
> raising a structure that was never planned.

I kiss the book.

*

It's nearing fall. They will be gathering for the flight
south—Snow Buntings, *Plectrophenax nivalis*, Snow Bird,
Snow Lark Bunting, Snow Flake, and all its local names,
names I can't pronounce or will never know.

Audubon imagines that flight for us:

> Their wings seem scarcely able to support their
> exhausted, nay almost congealed bodies, which
> seem little larger than the great feathery flakes of
> the substance from which these delicate creatures
> have borrowed their name.

Do we share with these "delicate creatures" only the
strange will to go on? Or is there something more they can
show us, something that can make them seem almost
sacred? Jane Harrison writes (in *Themis*):

> Beasts and birds in their silent, aloof, goings, in
> the perfection of their limited doings are mysteri-
> ous still and wonderful. . . . Birds are not, never
> were, gods; there is no definite bird-cult, but there
> are an infinite number of bird-sanctities. Man in
> early days tries to bring himself into touch with
> bird-*mana*, he handles reverently bird-sanctities.

*

My granddaughter, just a year old, sits on the grass and follows the movements of a nearby Common Grackle—not a scarce bird where she lives in southeast Texas. I try to see the bird through her eyes. Impossible. How long will she possess this capacity for innocent wonder? Some never entirely lose it. Darwin, awed by what he has discovered, concludes *The Origin of Species* with this:

> There is grandeur in this view of life, with its several powers, having been originally breathed into a few forms or into one; and that, whilst this planet has gone cycling on according to the fixed law of gravity, from so simple a beginning endless forms most beautiful and most wonderful have been, and are being, evolved.

How easily the word "beautiful" glides off the tongue of the man who warned us not to let superficial appearance distract us from the truth of life, a heartless and unending struggle for existence.

Is it merely a matter of distance? From far-off: beautiful and wonderful forms in perpetual creative development. From close-up: "nature red in tooth and claw." And do we live in some middle distance where all extremes blur into one comfortable confusion?

*

We no longer have bird-sanctities. We have aviaries. And these too can have their beauty. Here is the historian Prescott on the magnificent aviary of the Aztec capital:

> There were, also, edifices appropriated to objects of quite another kind. One of these was an immense aviary, in which birds of splendid plumage were assembled from all parts of the empire. Here was the scarlet cardinal, the golden pheasant, the endless parrot-tribe with their rainbow hues, (the royal green predominant,) and that miniature miracle of nature, the humming-bird, which delights to revel among the honeysuckle bowers of Mexico. Three hundred attendants had charge of this aviary, who made themselves acquainted with the appropriate food of its inmates, oftentimes procured at great cost, and in the moulting season were careful to collect the beautiful plumage, which, with its many-colored tints, furnished the materials for the Aztec painter.

But an aviary is merely an aviary, nothing sacred, and thus as susceptible to human savagery as any other human beauty:

> On the other side of the square, adjoining Montezuma's residence, were several buildings, as the reader is aware, appropriated to animals. One of these was now marked for destruction, — the House of Birds, filled with specimens of all the painted varieties which swarmed over the wide

forests of Mexico. It was an airy and elegant building, after the Indian fashion, and, viewed in connection with its object, was undoubtedly a remarkable proof of refinement and intellectual taste in a barbarous monarch. Its light, combustible materials of wood and bamboo formed a striking contrast to the heavy stone edifices around it, and made it obviously convenient for the present purpose of the invaders. The torches were applied, and the fanciful structure was soon wrapped in flames, that sent their baleful splendors, far and wide, over city and lake. Its feathered inhabitants either perished in the fire, or those of stronger wing, bursting the burning lattice-work of the aviary, soared high into the air, and fluttering for a while over the devoted city, fled with loud screams to their native forests beyond the mountains.

*

Is there such a thing as profane reverence? Or is it not just an oxymoron but a contradiction so gaping as to make it an impossibility? I watch birdwatchers wait in all weather and all hours, wait with patience that requires faith. And where there is faith, there is likely to be reverence. Today's faithful watchers are perhaps the modern equivalent of those ancients who handled "reverently bird-sanctities."

*

"But what, Leonard," Lewis asks, "do you *want* of birds?" He and I have been walking the park on the long ridge of hills above his house. Now we are sitting in the shade of an old oak, a massive tree, its thick lower limbs extending out almost horizontally, perhaps thirty feet or more. We are watching the chickadees feed high up in the canopy and three Dark-eyed Juncos almost at our feet, searching the cool dust for seeds. They are joined by a towhee, then another. A Steller's Jay scolds us from a branch just over our heads and a Song Sparrow is singing somewhere off to our left, a young bird judging from the tentativeness of its song.

We have been at it again, arguing over what birdwatching is really about. He, of course, is content to locate it in human psychology. I, of course, want more. I want to find in the experience a kind of knowledge difficult, perhaps impossible, to explain in words. I fetch up out of my pocket a scrap of paper and read him what I have copied from a book by George Steiner:

> In a wholly fundamental, pragmatic sense, the poem, the statue, the sonata are not so much read, viewed or heard as they are *lived*.

"Why can't it be so with birds?" I accompany my question with a sweeping gesture that sends the birds fluttering up into the leaves. We are silent awhile, long enough for one junco to regain its confidence and drop down again.

"Oh," says Lewis, "this one's different! It's of the Slate-colored subspecies; the rest I believe are Oregons. Of course, we'd have to do some serious work before we could say it's *hyemalis hyemalis* or another of the Slate-colored race. But how nice to have it dining practically at our feet."

He studies it awhile, then looks up with a big grin: "Does that qualify as an epiphany or is it just another tepid observation of a dry-as-dust ornithologist?"

*

We are like the fat boy in *The Pickwick Papers* who "wants to make your flesh creep." That is, Thursday's Children, sitting under a Bishop pine as beautifully distorted as a bonsai, are discussing world ecology and its impact on birds. We each have a candidate for villain in the apparent falling-off of bird populations—slaughter of the rain forests, greenhouse effect, El Niño, acid rain, gaps or thinning in the ozone layer, changes in our own environment that are unfavorable to some birds (we care for) like warblers, and favorable to some (we don't care for) like Starlings, House Sparrows, blackbirds, cowbirds. One of our number even argues that nature is, to some degree and often with human help, doing bad things to itself. Acid rain, we are told, preceded our presence, and volcanic eruptions can have baleful effects on the whole world.

We can even imagine an earth more desolate than Isaiah foretold, as he envisaged the consequences of the Lord's wrath at the nations: "the cormorant and the bittern shall possess it; the owl also and the raven shall dwell in it: and he shall stretch out upon it the line of confusion, and the stones of emptiness." In our future world, humans will do the possessing and the dwelling, but without birds. We shall have driven out or killed the cormorant and bittern, the owl and even the resilient raven. We will wake up one morning to an empty and silent sky and only then learn the meaning of song and flight.

We are, of course, performing a ritual with this sort of conversation. In part it is our fear talking in the tones of rational speculation and high-minded indignation. Putting the evil we perceive into words seems to make it a little less overwhelming. Our incredulity also speaks, a disbelief that anything so momentous could happen to us, decent keepers of the law and unselfish lovers of nature.

Suddenly, Abel, who has been paying no attention to all this scary talk—perhaps because he has his hearing aid turned off—calls our attention to a Downy Woodpecker in the pine next to ours. We are more than usually pleased. The spell has been broken, the ritual deferred by real presence. Our tone becomes lighter. Lighter and more personal.

Later, though, I wonder if, in our sense of powerlessness before the vast forces around us, we had too easily slipped into the Here and Now. Is it a kind of selfishness to take refuge in the present? And so exclusive and benign-seeming a present?

*

Wondering is a kind of wandering, and on certain gray mornings I can almost imagine myself another man—the old monk, say, in the poem by Wang Yang-ming. He wakes at dawn to bird cries and his sleep is "companion / of the sleep of tigers." If I keep my eyes closed, I can hear wind in the pine and bamboo that hide his shack in their shadows.

*

Turning the pages of Armstrong's *The Folklore of Birds*, I come upon a print of Paleolithic Snowy Owls: a chick and its parents engraved on the stone wall of Trois Frères. The birds stare out at me, black eyes with white rings. Their stare is relentless, remote. It's only a few months ago I saw a living Snowy Owl and felt, if not kinship, something like warmth. But it was daylight and not far from human habitation. And it was my first look. The Trois Frères birds are of a different kind—long dead, their form only sketchily represented on stone in their tundra nest. But living and dead share one thing: the relentless stare, a stare from beyond kinship, beyond warmth, from an otherness never, it seems, to be approached. The pictured birds seem to be the eerie negatives of the living bird in my memory. The artist who put these birds on stone understood very well that what he represented was as alien as the rock that was his ground.

*

I'm out early, alone. A male Vermilion Flycatcher was spotted yesterday in the willows by East Beach. I scan the trees, but no flycatcher. I hear someone come up beside me. It's Dan. We exchange greetings and speculate on the whereabouts of the bird. A third watcher, a stranger, joins us long enough to say that he saw the bird yesterday morning but has heard that it was spooked later in the day by a noisy group of picnickers nearby. Dan and I persist awhile, our eyes searching the leaves, although we agree that there is little likelihood of the bird's returning.

I mention to Dan that this would have been a first for me. He, of course, has seen the bird many times but never minds seeing it again, particularly out of its normal range.

"Why out of its normal range?" I ask.

"Maybe because you see it better that way. Maybe you see a bird more sharply where you don't expect it, where it doesn't belong. It's sort of like seeing it for the first time again."

I have never heard Dan say so much at one time. And what he has to say pleases me. I lower my binoculars and turn to thank him, but he is gone, or rather, become a diminishing, solitary figure walking away under gulls out and toward the beach. Maybe I have been hasty in counting him among the fanatic listers. Reverence, like love, can take many forms.

*

Lewis is reserved about his fieldwork. When he speaks of it, he speaks in generalities. It is not shyness, but professional reticence. I am an outsider, one who would require a lot of explanation—and to no serious end, probably to feed a momentary burst of curiosity. But once, not long ago, I winkled some details out of him by making just the right request.

"Lewis, take me out on your next field trip."

Lewis picks his pipe up, thrusts it in his mouth and stares at me. Am I serious? Finally, he shakes his head and says, "You'd be bored stiff with the drill out there, and the weather would floor you, 110 in the shade."

"What do you do? I mean, what's the routine?"

"Well, it depends." He seems to relax his guard a little as he speaks. "There are different procedures for different studies. One kind might require that we stay put in a blind for a certain period. Another, that we zone off areas and divide them among ourselves. Say I take three, one zone a day. I walk very slowly from one end to the other, then double back to catch what I may have missed, recording data the whole time."

"What kind?"

"Oh, the usual—behavior patterns of my birds and any apparent anomalies. I'll record data on their arrivals and departures, their flocking, pairing, courtship, nest making, songs and calls—that sort of thing. Not too exciting, eh? But these are the dry little scribbles that can add up to real knowledge about the world."

"Why do you do it?"

"Why?" Lewis leans back in his chair, sucks on his pipe, and lets his eyes wander to the ceiling. "That's a good question. I *could* say that it's a matter of temperament, which is true. I *like* to observe things closely and try to figure out why they do what they do. But it's more than that, I think. When I was a boy, collecting butterflies and plant specimens, I already had this vague but urgent notion that if I could know one part of the universe, however small, I could understand the whole of it."

"And do you? Do you understand the whole of it?"

"Oh, I couldn't say. I'm still trying to understand some of the parts.

"Listen," Lewis says, as if waking from reverie, "you just go out to the banding station. Spend a day with the people out there. That'll give you some idea of what professionals do without your having to learn the hard way."

*

Home, I open to a poem of Tennyson. How many years since I read—and dismissed—it?

> Flower in the crannied wall,
> I pluck you out of the crannies;—
> Hold you here, root and all, in my hand,
> Little flower—but if I could understand
> What you are, root and all, and all in all,
> I should know what God and man is.

In this small, slightly discolored mirror I think I see the face of my friend Lewis, the tough-minded, matter-of-fact ornithologist.

*

I arrive at the station early, too early. It's still shut. I walk around, practicing the mien of sober attentiveness proper to the on-duty ornithologist—precisely the wrong attitude, I find when I introduce myself to the student-staff. They are all very young, at the beginning of their careers in the field, young and full of generous high spirits. They are happy to invite me to walk out to the nets with them and help untangle any birds that have been caught for banding. I can watch them examine, then band the netted birds. And I can ask them any questions I'd like. Norma, a tall, willowy Oregonian with loose brown hair hanging to her shoulders, already calls me by my first name, as though none of us has any other.

Our first trip to the nets gets us one bird, a Ruby-crowned Kinglet (which I have trouble identifying at first, never having seen the bird four inches from my nose). Lisa, a sturdy, deeply tanned young woman from Michigan, releases it from the net and puts it in a little cloth bag. She has a big ready laugh and makes terrible bird puns. (When is a swallow not a swallow? When it's a gulp, dummy.) I ask her if she thinks the bird, which makes no stir in the bag, is terrified. She doesn't think so. "It depends on the bird, but if we're very gentle with them, they seem, well, accepting."

"Is that a good idea—for them?"

"I don't understand."

"Forget it. Neither do I."

The banding room, next to the little museum of stuffed birds of the area, is also the visitors' reception room. Here, Lisa goes to work on our specimen: weight, dimensions, sex, age, general condition, all recorded in a big gray ledger on the counter behind which Lisa works. She is gentle and talks to the bird in a soft voice, praising it, assuring it. I try to read its eyes but meet only with a stare of opaque intensity—the gaze perhaps of a creature that lives its life much more swiftly than we live ours. Finally, the now-banded kinglet is released through a small opening in the wall to the left of the counter.

Between trips to the nets, time drags a little, only partially quickened by banter and my questions. Trying to hide a yawn, I ask if it is part of the nature of their work that it should now and then seem tedious (I am thinking of Lewis tramping up and down his zones in the blazing desert heat). Zach, an Indianan, tall enough for basketball, answers for all of them, judging from the vigorous nods of approval that accompany his comments. They may joke, but they're serious.

"Not really. There's always something to do, something more to learn. But you have to love what you're doing."

Out to the nets again, this time with four birds in them: a Golden-crowned Sparrow, a Western Wood-Pewee, a Chestnut-backed Chickadee, and, the prize, a Townsend's

Warbler, not rare but pretty, always a pleasure to see. We free the birds, bag them, and bring them in.

One at a time they are examined, banded, and released. We lean in to watch Barry, who is very proficient, at work on the Townsend's. As Zach is very tall, so Barry is very short. They are too young to remember Mutt and Jeff, but are nevertheless jokingly paired off.

I wonder aloud how it feels holding a bird and I am handed, then and there, the Townsend's with brief instructions on how it should be held. I feel its pulse, and my own heart beats faster. I remember the bird that died so many years back in this same—but not same—hand. I give the Townsend's, a little abruptly, back to Barry, who looks a question at me. "Strange," I say in reply. "It felt strange," and hope he will not ask in what way.

He says only, "You get used to it."

And so it goes until I thank my hosts and drive off. All the way home, I try to make something of the experience. But it remains unyieldingly itself. Even the feel of the bird in my palm suggests nothing and I hear myself saying, impatiently, "Let it be. Let it be."

*

Thursday's Children have come a long way to see Mountain Plovers. The weather has turned against us, billows of fog rolling across the slopes where our birds are supposed to be foraging. It's not yet noon and we all have our car lights on. Like the weather, the mood is drab and cheerless as we pull over and park on the side of the road, getting out for a better look. Our eyes sweep over the lower slopes, where the fog is a little thinner. Nothing.

Suddenly a big bird comes gliding out of the fog, a hawklike bird hard to make out against the gray background. Then three voices go up like a chorus: "Peregrine Falcon!" Naomi, Abel, and Dan have given the bird its proper name. The bird glides low overhead and we get a clear view of its black "sideburns," its brilliant eye. It banks, circling right and back toward the fog. Then it's gone, leaving behind a changed group. We are not grumbling now or behaving as though our hearts were buried in fog. We are exultant in a modest way, ready for all opportunities, game for any chance.

*

When a non-birdwatcher friend wonders if birdwatchers, so wrapped up in their eccentricity, have any sense of humor, I say sure they do and give her an example.

One day the group noticed Dan walking toward us in the company of a young woman. He had been birdwatching on his own for a couple of months. We asked the usual question, "Seen anything good?"

He shook his head, "Not yet." We had exchanged a couple of minutes of this and that when he turned to the young woman and said, "This is Gaya," after which the two drifted off.

"It must be love," Ursula said.

Claire asked why.

"She wasn't wearing binoculars."

My friend stares at me blankly.

*

Lewis has a remarkable ear; he can hear and identify bird-calls over extraordinary distances. I ask him if long-range naming gives him the same pleasure as seeing the bird itself. He does not reply immediately. We are sitting on the veranda, watching birds at the feeder I have set up near the back fence. Mostly House Finches, but also some chickadees and a skittish nuthatch. His gaze still fixed on the feeder, Lewis finally says, "It's hearing a distant trumpet before you see its blaze."

I put this comparison down to Lewis's love of opera, but say only, "Why, Lewis, you've committed a metaphor."

"Oh, come on! It's no great news that science uses metaphor." This is said with a tinge of impatience. "May I remind you that *electron* anciently meant 'strange force'."

"So does heart. What's the difference?"

"For one thing, scientific metaphors are usually, for the sake of stability, dead ones. I would think that you poets would prefer yours live."

"What do you say to *quark*?"

Now Lewis turns to me, grinning: "What's in a name?"

A Scrub Jay chooses just this moment to land at the feeder, drive the other birds off and, between savage pecks at the seed, scold us who mean it no harm.

Lewis says, "Scarlatti."

It takes me awhile to pick up, through all the other sounds, faint music from a distant radio.

*

I have dreamt often the last few days. Most of it was banal and blurry surrealism. One dream was clear—a man standing alone in a vast field. He has his back to me; then, very slowly, he turns. The face is too familiar for surprise, but the eyes are the eyes of a bird, perhaps a falcon.

*

You were not there—none of us was—
that dawn last fall when he started a bird
out of stubble at Far Corners,
where—as he tells it—the squawk
and uprush under his feet froze him
in place so when he got the binoculars
up to his eyes, the bird had almost
made the far edge of the field,
made it and made the slope beyond,

a small and smaller trace of white
fluttering over the new-plowed earth,
then a mote in the sky, and then
nothing but the vast pallor
of palpable distance, at which he stared
long after he had lowered,
slowly, the binoculars
like an offering refused, feeling
himself—daft as it seemed—refused,
denied, as though the damned bird,
denying him simple recognition,
denied also—and here he blushed
in the telling—a foolish hope, dead,
he thought, all these years, hope
for a sign that there was more to it
than nature red in tooth and claw,
hope for a sign of recognition
from the other side—hope
of an old doubter who reads his grandson
fables where the beasts reply
in human voices even his grandson
knows are heard only in books,
but there he stood still hoping,
still hopeless, like a man
at the center of an ever-widening,
all-consuming circle of sadness
that all creatures instinctively flee,
so that if, now, he turned, ran toward the road,
crawled through the fence, got in his car,
drove hard to the nearest town,

he'd be too late, find it forsaken,
coffee cups half empty,
sweet rolls bitten into, warm
still to the touch, newspapers
spread to read, their readers gone,
the dogs gone, leaving him
a world still warm, its sweetness
bitten into, sweetness he could
all but taste, so real it seemed,
or was, and he had to shake his head
to break the charm, and did, waking
in the field as much alone
as ever, but now his heart beat
against its cage, his skin shivered
with a panic sweat as he stared
wildly around at things as they are,
and last fall they were gorgeous—
a long, slow recessional
of heartfelt greens dying ripely
into burnt yellows, themselves
dying into silver ash,
the air scented with the smoke
of remote fires, damp hay, gusts
of fine rain, an air as close
to flesh as it could ever come
if touching only to say good-bye,
and when he looked up, he saw good-bye
also in the high migration
of geese, felt the tug of it,
so elemental you could trace

its trail on cave walls or tablets
of crumbling clay, another tale
to read his grandson. In this one, the hero
sets out on a road mapped in dreams,
and after many kinds of death,
he finds, only to lose again,
yet finds, in losing, something else:
not gold or the galling aftertaste
of immortality, but precious
still, too late of course to save
an old man so easily
distracted from (or by) essentials—
as there, off to his right, a harrier
gliding low and unhurried over
the dumb terror of mice, or the sound
of a car at his back, so he turned around
and saw it park in front of his,
a woman climb out, slip between strands
of barbed wire, and come toward him,
waving—friend or stranger?—he couldn't
make out as he waited to exchange
rumors of rare things seen
or heard, the ceremonial gossip
of their hobby—less a hobby,
his wife would tease, more an obsession—
and, of course, she was right, and now
he saw her before him in a sort
of lay epiphany, moving
briskly about the bright kitchen,
cup in hand as she hummed to herself,

thinking her own thoughts, ones
he'd never perhaps hear, or hear
wrong because that old bird,
his mind, half-deaf anyhow,
seemed to listen more and more
to a call just beyond his hearing,
wandered more and more, sometimes
simply in search of where he was,
as here on this field, breathing
the musk of ready earth as he waited
for one of his own kind to arrive,
slowly, out of immense absence,
one solitude waiting
on another, and why not?—
for wasn't waiting the one office,
all the others having failed,
the old decently could do?—
and here—why not?—he smiled a little
and waved back, though tentatively,
like a man who didn't much trust
his eyes, but squinting a little, saw
it wasn't anyone he knew.

*

In this dream, all the true and secret names of the birds are
entered in the sacred book. As I read down the page, I gasp;
everything is revealed in these names. Everything! But there
is one condition to be observed: It is forbidden to remem-

ber the contents of these pages when the book is closed, and I wake unconsoled to light and the piercing cry of a Red-tailed Hawk.

＊

You learn to be grateful for field guides—and learn also to mistrust them taken one by one. You learn to be grateful because you don't have to reinvent all the birds each time you go out. Or memorize worlds of information and reams of pictures. It's all there condensed in one small volume that will fit in a big pocket or a small tote bag. Your gratitude will be all the greater if you look through an old black-and-white guide. A bird world without color! Unimaginable.

But for all this gratitude, in practice you get cagey. You do not use only one guide. Two are better because one can sometimes compensate for the deficiencies of the other. Three can be even better, enabling you to cross reference the bird, to come a little closer to its reality perhaps. But that reality is so complex and shifting that no book, no calculable number of books, can grasp it. It consists of a bird, unique as a snowflake, in one of its many stages of life. It is sitting at one angle or another or flying in one direction or another. The bird's background is light or dark, wind-shaken or still. It is perching, if it is perching, high or low and at any one of 360 degrees and any distance away to the end of visibility.

A book is a poor static simplification of these matters. And every bird in it, if photographed, is not your bird, because the photographed bird is only that bird—as unique as a snowflake. If done by hand, the bird is not your bird because it will be a universal or ideal version of your bird.

But you also learn not to despair. Now and then you may even find a perfect match between bird and book. All doubt is then dispelled like the fog that so hindered your seeing. All is bright and sunshiny and the way it should be. You feel a deep satisfaction. Not quite epiphany perhaps, but good enough.

Books, good books, are ambivalent, pulling you away from your life, pushing you into it, often at one and the same time.

＊

If a student of the Torah reads the scriptures with requisite concentration—concentration like pure passion—the Hebrew letters of the text will lift from the page and, becoming birds, circle over his head, spelling out the many names of God, and even, on rare occasions, the unpronounceable hidden one.

Did I invent this out of misremembering something told me? Or did I find it in some book I have long forgotten?

＊

Tuesday: The phone rings me out of sleep just after dawn. Spencer—our group's contact man—tells me a Connecticut Warbler has been spotted at Long Bay at such and such a place. I'm there / here two hours later and am the sole representative of Thursday's Children among the dozen watchers. I have reviewed the bird over five gulps of coffee—a plumpish species with grayish green back, yellowish undersides, and a distinct ring around a big black eye. It walks mincingly along the ground, from time to time flitting up to catch an insect. I think I'm ready.

We straggle up a creek-side trail not very far before someone ahead shouts, "There it is!" and points down at the almost dry creek bed about twenty-five feet below us and to our right. There it is indeed, just as the books almost had it. It minces, it flits up, it is gray and yellow, all assembled into a whole bird.

It's a rarity out here and a first for me. I'm deeply satisfied. After a good long look, I make way for others eager for the same. A man is setting up camera gear. He smiles as I pass him. Everyone is in glowing good spirits. It has been such an easy bird—a pleasant drive, a brief walk, an unimpeded view, and now home in time for lunch.

So why am I discontented? Perhaps because the experience has demanded so little of me. Or because I had looked so hard at the books I couldn't get free of their pictures and saw the bird through them. It seems that I have had a recognition without the shock. Satisfaction, however deep, is probably not epiphany.

When Thursday's Children—none of whom had reached the place before the bird flew—asked me about my seeing the warbler, I was nonchalant. "Nice," I said, "very nice," knowing full well that they thought I was understating the case. This once I wasn't.

*

As some people play bridge or pinochle, a few friends and I compose parables. The one rule of this game is that these inventions must give the appearance of wisdom but in fact defy sense. I am challenged to compose one that had a bird in it. This is one I give them:

> The Master of Dwalno was standing in the doorway of the sanctum when a bird, a magpie, landed on his left shoulder. His disciples, alarmed, asked what this signified; and he, calming them, said, "I have just received an answer to a question I have not yet asked."

It is unanimously agreed that this parable perfectly meets the rule. After my friends have gone, however, I find myself trying to make sense of it, feeling that I am on the verge of doing so. But it is only the verge of sleep.

*

I dream of the sacred book; I know I will find in it the following—another account by the Italian traveler.

On his way to visit the court of the emperor of the Germans, Stampari stopped at a village inn. There, as he sat over his tankard, he heard a strange story from a man dressed in the garb of a scholar, Ulrich by name.

It seemed that a rich peasant who owned land near the village was in the habit, weather permitting, of riding at dusk the whole circumference of a large lake that was part of his holdings. This he always did alone, being a solitary, unsociable man. One especially bitter February day, the lake frozen over, he was about halfway in his ride when he saw a swan sitting on the ice, so draggled and droopy that it must have been sick or exhausted. Migrating flocks were passing overhead, leaving it behind.

The peasant rode back to his barn, fetched a big sack, and hitched his horse to a small cart, climbed in, and rode back to the lake. Capturing the bird in its weakened state was easy. He then stuffed it into the sack and took it to his henhouse, where he called out to a servant of his, one Kurl, to help him unload the bird. Kurl imagined that his master had taken the bird to eat.

But late that night, the servant was wakened by his master's muttering and thumping. Then he heard the front door open and shut very softly. He naturally became curious, rose, and slipped out the door, tiptoeing after his master, who held a small lantern up to the dark. Then he saw, and heard, an amazing thing. When his master opened the henhouse door, the swan, in the lovely voice of a girl, begged him to release her from her wretched little dungeon, promising, if he did, that she would change into a beautiful woman and become his devoted wife. Just then Kurl was overcome by the need to sneeze. When it came, his master whirled, seized him by the throat, and promised to kill him if ever he let drop a word about what had just transpired.

"Here!" he snarled, handing Kurl a pouch heavy with gold. "Go spend it in some other village. Understand?"

Kurl nodded and slunk off—not to another village, but to the inn of his own, where he didn't exactly tell what he had seen but hinted that something very odd was going on at his master's. People wondered about Kurl's sudden fortune, but because he was more often drunk than sober, paid him no further mind.

Until, that is, the rich peasant suddenly left town and returned shortly with a beautiful bride, half his age and as delicate and ladylike as he was squat and coarse. Kurl was now listened to and, drunk, blurted out the whole story. Still no one believed him. Villagers decided instead that the peasant had gone off to the city and bought himself a wife from some bankrupt aristocratic family. No one dared ask the peasant, known for his ferocious temper, and no one was invited to his house to have a close look at the new bride.

Time passed and children were seen from a distance riding ponies in a field by the rich man's house. And then one day, as Kurl, on his way to the inn, passed the lake, something lying in his path stopped him in midstride: silken garments, white as snow, all stacked in three neat piles, one much larger than the other two. Each consisted of a dress, shift, and stockings, and a pair of slim white sandals sat on the top of each heap. And even more puzzling, seven or eight long white feathers were scattered around the heaps. He scooped all this up in his arms and began to run toward the peasant's house; from where else could such stuff have come? But suddenly he stopped, reflected a little, then decided that, since he had revealed all he knew, his ex-master might well keep his promise to kill him or at least give him a sound thrashing for his trouble.

Instead, he ran to the inn and showed his prize to the proprietor and to the three or four guests who sat at the tables drinking. What to do? The proprietor scratched his head. Finally he decided it was *his* duty to take the articles to the peasant (not to mention the possibility of a reward). This he did, handing them over to the peasant, who was so red and swollen that the proprietor hurriedly backed away, afraid the man would explode. Suddenly the peasant fell to the ground and buried his face in the silks, sobbing and groaning, "Oh, little Olora! Oh, my heart's treasure! You warned me. You did. And yet this is too hard. You said, 'Jakob, strike me, and I will instantly change back into a swan—the children too! You will never, never see us again.' You warned me. I admit it. But oh, this is too hard. And it was not me, but the drink, my little Olora. And the children, my two beautiful daughters, such ladies, so loving. I am being paid back for my pride. But it's too much. I cannot bear it." Here, the proprietor left, embarrassed by the scene and saddened too.

The story is soon ended. The bereaved man spent the rest of his days—which were not many—scanning the sky for his lost beloved. And when a flight of swans went by, he would cry out to them, hoping one might be she, but always they all flew on. It is said that to this day they no longer land on the lake, as they had before, to rest.

When Stampari asked Ulrich if there was any evidence for this marvel, the scholar called to a shapeless figure in a dark corner of the inn. It was no other than Kurl, smelling of beer, filth, and sweat. Ulrich said something to him, and the wretch reached into the pocket of his greasy sheepskin jacket and produced a long white feather, or what once was a white feather. Now it was smudged and rumpled with much handling by dirty hands.

Stampari writes: I took it from him, turned it over, and said to Ulrich, as I handed it back to Kurl, that I did not find this "evidence" of a kind that would convince reasonable men. Then, to my amazement, Kurl, clutching the feather to his chest, began to weep. So too did the rough old proprietor and also three men seated at a table, hunched over their tankards.

I then asked Ulrich if *he* gave this tale any credence. He smiled and shrugged. I then asked him what sort of scholar he was.

"A scholar of metamorphosis," he replied.

"Metamorphosis?" I repeated.

"Yes," he nodded. "It is my belief that if we can understand change, we can understand everything."

"What do you make of *this* metamorphosis?" I asked.

"Tears, unforced tears, are strong proof of something."
As he said this, he rose, bowed, and walked out of the room.

It was at this moment, writes Stampari, that I felt a penetrating chill in one hand. When I looked down, I saw it was the hand that had held the feather. The sensation lasted for an hour and a half and has never recurred.

*

Three friends, one after the other, call to tell me about a new book on birds in literature, and that I might be especially interested in a poem it contains, Whitman's "Of That Blithe Throat of Thine." I thank them, exchange news, ring off. I assume that the poem is about the Snow Bunting and sit awhile trying to imagine how it will unfold. I don't recall ever having read it. I am in no hurry to get down Whitman, fearing perhaps that expectation will overshoot reality. But he is full of surprises. Finally, I pull the volume out of its place, find the page, and open to this:

Of That Blithe Throat of Thine

(MORE THAN EIGHTY-THREE DEGREES NORTH—
ABOUT A GOOD DAY'S STEAMING DISTANCE TO
THE POLE BY ONE OF OUR FAST OCEANERS IN
CLEAR WATER—GREELY THE EXPLORER HEARD THE
SONG OF A SINGLE SNOW-BIRD MERRILY SOUNDING
OVER THE DESOLATION)

Of that blithe throat of thine from arctic bleak and blank,
I'll mind the lesson, solitary bird—let me too welcome
    chilling drifts,
E'en the profoundest chill, as now—a torpid pulse, a brain
    unnerv'd,
Old age land-lock'd within its winter bay—(cold, cold, O
    cold!)
These snowy hairs, my feeble arm, my frozen feet,
For them thy faith, thy rule I take, and grave it to the last;
Not summer's zones alone—not chants of youth, or
    south's warm tides alone,
But held by sluggish floes, pack'd in the northern ice, the
    cumulus of years,
These with gay heart I also sing.

This is disappointing. I look in vain for the bird as bird. I wanted some reaching out to otherness, some living contact with a reality beyond us. Instead, I get bird—and very little bird at that—as teacher. I wanted epiphany and I get a lesson.

The prose of Nethersole-Thompson does more justice to the Snow Bunting. Singing "its wild sweet notes," it seems to him "sometimes the only triumphant challenge of life in an almost dead arctic world," and this scrupulously objective scientist confesses, "I always thrill when I hear the snow bird sing in some distant misty corrie."

I put the poem aside and go on to other business.

*

The message of the latest postcard is the briefest yet: "Bird anthology — yours?" I turn the card over, expecting to find a brilliant cardinal or elegant flamingo, but find instead a pre–Civil War railway engine. It is as bright and colorful as a toy. Its brass gleams as though it were set in place this morning. Those who built it were still optimists and cherished their materials as artists cherish theirs.

As to the anthology of bird poems, I think not. But there's no harm in playing with the notion. I would have most of the poems be brief and concentrated in the way epiphanies are brief and concentrated. I would exclude poems in which the birds were coddled singers for their supper or caged mimics of human speech. The first poem in the book — a little long, I admit — would be from a book of verses for children, composed by the author of *The Pilgrim's Progress*, John Bunyan. It is called "Of the Child with the Bird at the Bush," and it warns precisely against the use of pet birds:

> My little bird, how canst thou sit
>   And sing amidst so many thorns?
> Let me but hold upon thee get,
>   My love with honour thee adorns.
>
> Thou art at present little worth,
>   Five farthings none will give for thee;
> But prithee, little bird, come forth,
>   Thou of more value art to me.

'Tis true it is sun-shine to-day,
　To-morrow birds will have a storm;
My pretty one, come thou away,
　My bosom then shall keep thee warm.

Thou subject art to cold o' nights,
　When darkness is thy covering;
At days thy danger's great by kites,
　How canst thou then sit there and sing?

Thy food is scarce and scanty too,
　'Tis worms and trash which thou dost eat;
Thy present state I pity do,
　Come, I'll provide thee better meat.

I'll feed thee with white bread and milk,
　And sugar-plums, if them thou crave;
I'll cover thee with finest silk,
　That from the cold I may thee save.

My father's palace shall be thine,
　Yea, in it thou shalt sit and sing;
My little bird, if thou 'lt be mine,
　The whole year round shall be thy spring.

I'll teach thee all the notes at court;
　Unthought-of music thou shalt play;
And all that thither do resort
　Shall praise thee for it every day.

I'll keep thee safe from cat and cur,
　No manner o' harm shall come to thee:

Yea, I will be thy succourer,
    My bosom shall thy cabin be.

But lo! behold, the bird is gone;
    These charmings would not make her yield:
The child's left at the bush alone,
    The bird flies yonder o'er the field.

*

"But you know," Lewis says, "it always seems to come back to what is *true* knowledge. When I speak of true knowledge, I am — in my profession — understood to mean a very specific thing, say, the structure of a bird's wing or the chemistry of its eggs.

"And please, Leonard, don't tell me about the slippage between things and words. We aren't naive. We know perfectly well that our names for things never can quite reflect their dynamic complexity. But we have methods for correcting slippage: We can test our ideas of what things are by experiment. We can measure, weigh, compare, all with a high degree of precision and a decent certainty that we can get our ideas about things closer to the things themselves.

"But when you talk about true knowledge, I find my mind wandering. And wondering. You claim for poetry some special kind of knowledge that has to be experienced. I can only suppose you mean something like intuitive knowledge. But how vague that really is, yet sometimes you seem to be saying that your kind of true knowledge is the only, or at least, the better true knowledge.

"But take your Snow Bunting. You can only claim to see it from the outside. You see its superficial qualities and declare it beautiful. I can do much more. I can know the wondrous mechanism that gives it its flight. I can go deeper, into its genetic character, the marvelous way its cells reproduce. And I bring all this to the experience of the wild bird, while all you have is its visible characteristics seen at a distance and under uncontrolled circumstances.

"So how can you talk about *true* knowledge, let alone a kind of knowledge that is superior or even equal to mine?"

I go to my study and find the book I want, come downstairs to the front room where Lewis sits, open the book, and read:

The View from Here
BY WILLIAM STAFFORD

In Antarctica drooping their little shoulders
like bottles the penguins stand, small,
sad, black — and the wind
bites hard over them.

Edging that continent they huddle to turn their eyes.
Penguins, we can't help you; and all that cold
hangs over us too, wide beyond thought.
We too stand and wait.

Lewis looks puzzled. "I don't understand."

"Evidence," I say. "Evidence for a true knowledge different from yours, leaving aside questions of superiority."

"How can a poem be evidence for knowledge about a bird?"

"Let me put it this way: The birds that you weigh and measure are different birds from Stafford's penguins, in and out of his poem. Your birds are specimens, cases, not individual presences. Poetry is a means for summoning that presence into language, for giving it perhaps a more intense meaning without losing its individuality for us. Like the bird itself, poetry can shock us into recognition of what we share with otherness; in this instance, an utter helplessness before the overwhelming forces of nature, but helplessness that evokes a compassion linking us even more closely to the birds."

"How you juggle words!" Lewis takes his pipe out of his mouth and examines its stem. No, it isn't chewed through yet. Time to go before the next bite.

*

Stafford's poem belongs in my anthology. So too does "Nightbird," from the Norwegian poet Rolf Jacobsen (translated by Roger Greenwald):

> Crows are the birds of night.
> Ponderously, out of the dawn, they come

> and guard us with anthracite eyes
> all day and with harsh calls,
> so we won't lose ourselves in the light.
> Heavy shadows over the roofs,
> dark wings on the windowpanes
> tie the threads
> from night to night.

These are first cousins to Eiseley's crow, agents of primal terror.

*

> [It] is, I believe, poetry, art and music which relate
> us most directly to that in being which is not ours.
> Science is no less animate in its making of models
> and images. But these are not, finally, disinter-
> ested. They aim at mastery, at ownership.

These words from George Steiner's *Real Presences* could have helped me against Lewis's big guns. A finch in flight or a shrike on a fence post is precisely "being which is not ours."

*

Thursday's Children are out in search of the Black Rail. I am in bed with a fever. The day is a slow river of dreamy misery, studded with little islands of lucidity. I am in a canoe or raft threading my way through a tropical marsh. Prehistoric flying reptiles rise out of the miasma and, screaming, circle my head. Someone is with me and not with me. I am escaping and pursuing. It begins to rain a steamy rain.

My wife wakes me, bringing in a tray with a bowl of broth and a cup of herbal tea. My bedclothes are drenched with sweat; the fever seems to have broken, the aches abated.

But I feel—what? Remorse. It takes me awhile to locate its cause. When I do, I am surprised—Whitman. Or Whitman's verses on the Snow Bunting. I ask my wife to bring me my copy of his poems and thumb through to the one in question. I read it. Reread it. Read it again.

Is it the weakness left by fever that makes me feel that I have done an injustice—if not to Whitman the poet, to Whitman the man? For the poem moves me now. Perhaps it is sickness calling out to sickness that makes me see that the moralizing I had found objectionable in my first reading is less important than the painful integrity that went so uneasily into these lines. I think I now glimpse a sad courage in the poet's faith that there is good reason to affirm life in the midst of suffering. For the evidence of that faith is a secondhand experience of a bird he himself will never hear or see. And isn't there also a desperate honesty in his treatment of the bunting, an honesty that admits, with such modest indirection, how little of the poet's energy was left to perform his appointed task. The bird is reduced to a throat, the poet to a song.

I ask my wife if what I now see in the poem is really there, but drift into sleep before she finishes her answer.

*

I have been staring out over a marshy pond for hours through rain and sun, watching for the Little Stint reportedly seen here yesterday. I am not alone. This is a very rare bird and has drawn two dozen or so birdwatchers standing beside their scopes, conversing in low voices. I ask the watcher on my right, a sharp-eyed, retired English professor, if he has seen the bird before. He has, once, and at a great distance. I ask him if seeing it now would be as great a thrill as the first sighting. He shrugs. A long silence ensues.

But the need to test my ideas, particularly with experienced birdwatchers, overcomes my shyness. So I put to him my notion of epiphany. For the first time he looks at me attentively, smiles a skeptical smile, and says that one might hope for such an experience once or twice in a lifetime.

This is disheartening. I imagine a ladder, its bottom rung commonplace notice, its highest rung true epiphany. Between lie all the possible degrees of seeing (and not seeing). Am I going to end up with a system too complicated and fragile to be of any use? Am I going to become another list maker, but of kinds and degrees of birdwatching experiences?

The stint never shows and the watchers fold up their scopes and drift off in twos and threes, toward the parking lot, my neighbor to the right among them. But as he turns to go, he looks over his shoulder and says, "Maybe the term *intimation* would be closer to what you're looking for."

Then he moves off, inviting no response. I stand there a long time, alone now, considering.

Home again, I open my Webster's and find a fruitful contradiction. *Intimation* can signify a proclamation, formal notice, or announcement. But it can also signify a hint, obscure or indirect suggestion, or notice. Am I wrong to find in these definitions a convergence or meeting of two opposing realms of experience: the objective thing-in-itself and its implications only intuited as a promise of more meaning?

My wife, as she thumbs through a recipe book, listens to all this and says, without looking up, "You never will find just the right word."

And that is oddly comforting.

*

"Well, it's likely to sound harsher than I mean it to," says Lewis, studying the burnished bowl of his pipe.

"We're old friends, Lewis."

"Well, you won't care for it," he says, shrugging.

"Try me," I say, keeping in mind that 'try' can mean both 'test' and 'exasperate.'

"All right then, I just find it hard to . . . ummm . . . credit your theory, because you're a flawed advocate. I mean— and you have told me this yourself often enough—that you're not a very precise observer, a fact that would seem to compromise your value as a witness to epiphany. If we put your observation against that of someone who sees a bird more fully and accurately, which one are we to trust? It was you who admitted just yesterday that you had never noticed the gold wash on the breast of the Swainson's Thrush until someone pointed it out to you. If epiphany is the issue, wouldn't the person who saw that wash be a better witness to the real presence of the bird? Which makes me think that your shocks of recognition are the perfectly natural psychological excitement of a man with your temperament. It's *fun*, sometimes even thrilling, to see a new bird, but there's nothing you can do with that feeling, I'm afraid, except enjoy it." Lewis, who has been looking out the window during this speech, now turns to me with a deprecating smile.

I try to seem amused: "So you're telling me to stop fussing with theories and start having some good old-fashioned fun?"

"Something like that," he says, looking away again. He's trying to be Lewis the friend and Lewis the scientist at one and the same time. But at the moment he is Lewis the uncomfortable, wishing perhaps that he hadn't spoken out. Or perhaps hadn't spoken out so frankly.

"It's really OK, Lewis," I say. "What kind of theory—if that's what it is—would it be if it didn't leave itself open to legitimate doubt? And as to all these limits and deficiencies—they are never far from my mind. I try always to factor them into my thinking.

"And then, my situation may not be as hopeless as it

seems. Maybe you're talking quantity and I'm talking quality. The qualitative experience of a bird is not the quantitative one. Quantity has only to do with the number of features noted. I can imagine a watcher who can see and name you all the visible characteristics of a bird and feel nothing in doing so."

"But," says Lewis, the friend, reassured by my readiness to fight on, "*I* can imagine a watcher giving the wrong name to a bird because its gold wash was missed. Would this watcher's excitement be shock of recognition before real presence or psychological kick based on a patent error?"

"I don't deny that misidentification could undermine epiphany . . ."

"Could?" says Lewis, lifting an eyebrow.

"But," I continue, ignoring the thrust, "we live in a world where appearance and reality are in constant and confusing play. It's not surprising that all of us now and then mistake one for the other and can only hope to correct our error in time."

"Yes, of course," Lewis says, "but will the correction be most likely the result of vague personal intuition and luck or of a vigorously objective method?" Lewis sits back, satisfied he's scored a major point without hurting my feelings. His pipestem is saved, for now.

*

My wife on the phone is calling from a far-off friend's; she is well, hopes I am, is having a good time, and is vastly amused by something of Auden she has just read. "Listen: 'When I find myself in the company of scientists, I feel like a shabby curate who has strayed by mistake into a drawing room full of dukes.' Wonderful, isn't it? But maybe you ought not tell Lewis."

She laughs even as she says good-bye.

*

The message side of the postcard this time is blank. I turn it over: a print of van Gogh's *Wheatfield with Crows.* The familiar sky is inky blue except where two big clouds roil on the horizon. From the upper right the crows, tiny black scribbles, descend like bits of sky broken off and falling to meet the thick violence of upthrust golds and reds and greens. The world, it seems, is about to implode. The fact that the painter may have been half-maddened by what he saw—and saw as no other had ever seen before—does not mean that the painting is based on "patent error." But I hear Lewis's voice in my head: "Ah, but Leonard, there are seeings and there are seeings."

*

I phone my father, six hundred miles away. All he wants to know, at ninety-three, his short-term memory failing, is how I am. Once though, he surprises me: "You've really got me hooked on birds." He can see from his retirement-hotel window House Sparrows, Mourning Doves, Starlings, and crows. And, oh yes, they used to have a parrot in a glass cage at the entrance to the dining room.

*

Tolstoy, quoting some scholar's report: "All the Atzurs have died out, but there is a parrot here who knows a few words of their language."

*

It's autumn migration and watchers have much to see, mostly warblers, although in their duller fall plumage.

Thursday's Children, having already seen a Lark Bunting this chill and foggy morning, are positioned on both sides of a stand of Monterey cypresses, binoculars raised to the black canopy where movement has been noted. The fog has drained much of the color from the birds and they are so high up that likely only their undersides will show.

Gradually other watchers arrive and take up positions under the trees. I lower my binoculars to see if I know any of them and also to give my neck a rest. Everyone else seems to be concentrating on the birds and, suddenly, I feel alone or distanced from them, even members of my own group. My eyes stop at a man on the other side of the stand. He's a stranger to me, but a typical watcher, fiftyish, face weathered by sun and rain ("a well-documented face," as one friend said of another), his loose-fitting garb brown and gray as faded fall plumage. He wears a visored camouflage army cap, and I can see from where I stand that his binoculars show the shiny scratch marks of much use. About him there is an aura of self-containment, of his own purposive, competent, and stubborn actuality. I am utterly excluded and remote from his life, and, as I look from individual to individual, from the lives of all the others here, some not three feet from where I stand.

It is as though my mind were drifting in a sea of internal fog. It is as though all my own purposes were drained away by that fog as the outer fog has drained the colors from the birds. Epiphany, real presence, shock of recognition, reverence, intimations—all the poetic terms for hopeful intuitions, now seem empty, frivolous, wholly beside the point, naming only what my ignorance has projected.

Even while I am thinking all this, someone points up at what seems a little twitch of leaves flicked by wind—no, I'm told, it's a female Black-throated Blue Warbler. I sort of see it. But I can also hear (in my imagination) one of these watchers saying to another, "He doesn't understand. He just doesn't get it." And at this bad moment, I don't.

I have no heart for more watching today. I go through the motions, but without joy or even pleasure. I say to myself, "The poetry has gone out of it." But it's not that. It's the awareness that self-pity, what I am feeling now, is so powerful a drug. If I were a nineteenth-century poet, I would probably project the feeling onto a nightingale (confusing its sex) and be done with it. Simply imagining that makes me feel a little better.

*

Naomi calls in the evening with some bit of bird news, which, as she puts it, "surprised her attention"—a lovely phrase, and perhaps cleaner, clearer than the shock of recognition. At least, another, more modest way of putting the experience.

*

Vālmīki has returned, in a dream. He is seated, eyes shut, in the lotus position by a little fire, a shawl over his shoulders. His divine visitor has long since gone and his own disciple is curled in the all-consuming sleep of youth. The sage himself cannot sleep. He thinks of the long work stretching before him, the telling of the life and deeds of Rāma, the occupation of a lifetime. He is not daunted. With Brahma's help, he will bring it off. But he is a little cast down at having his life all set out for him, a fate as predictable as a ritual.

And another thought haunts him, one he tries to suppress because he knows it will distract him from the great task. Try as he may, however, the thought returns, fluttering in and out of his consciousness. And his poem, the first poem ever, sings itself over in his head, and the feelings that inspired it come back as he relives the strange experience of the morning—was it so short a time ago? But this won't do. He must give all his attention to the story of the god. And to that end, he begins to clear his mind, to expel all the vain events of the day from his awareness, until it is empty except for a crystalline pool under a willow whose shadow plays on the lit surface of the water. The tree must go next, leaving only a bottomless clarity, sweet and cool and utterly pure.

But the tree will not go. And in it he sees two birds—no, only one—he can't be sure and is deeply troubled. The pond grows murky, its face ruffled as though by wind. He is losing his concentration. Suddenly the bird screams and his heart stops, then leaps in his chest. He opens his eyes wide—nothing. It's the same small fire, dying now, the same disciple curled in sleep. The same Vālmīki, although he is least sure of that just now.

How long has he been asleep? How much of all this is a dream? And why is his heart still beating so hard?

*

Seen against a dark hillside or a lowering sky, a flock of these birds presents an exceedingly beautiful appearance, and it may then be seen how aptly the term "snowflake" has been applied to the species. I am acquainted with no more pleasing combination of sight and sound than that afforded when a cloud of these birds, backed by a dark grey sky, descends, as it were, in a shower to the ground, to the music of their own sweet tinkling notes.

These words are from the pen of one Dr. Saxby, quoted in Archibald Thorburn's *British Birds*. There may be a certain flowery stiffness in the style—the poetic voice of science?—but there is also genuine delight. Something in this small bird draws observers out—perhaps that "pleasing combination of sight and sound." Or perhaps it's the presence of so vital a life where no such life has any right to be. It is then Whitman's bird, singing sweet defiance against its bitter conditions, carrying the energy and beauty of living presence into the heart of desolation.

Surely, Dr. Saxby and Archibald Thorburn seem to say that if a bird can sing in polar ice, it can also sing in the somber haze of depression.

*

My wife reads anything that comes her way, including some things that fall out of the sky. She came in a few minutes ago, waving a book over her head, a medieval book of wonders. "I've found you the perfect birthday present," she says.

"What would that be?" I ask warily.

"A stone from India that, if it's put in a man's mouth, gives him the understanding of all birds!" We both laugh, but I think for different reasons.

*

22 September 1981, reprinted from the
San Francisco Chronicle:

MASS DEATH DIVES BY INDIAN BIRDS

New Delhi:— Hundreds of birds have committed "mass suicide" by smashing themselves against lamps, the United News of India reported yesterday.

Experts who are studying it are baffled by the phenomenon, observed in Haflong town in the northeastern state of Assam, about 1000 miles from New Delhi, and first noticed in 1905.

The birds repeatedly dive at night into glass-covered electric and kerosene outdoor lamps, frequently killing themselves on impact.

During the experts' three-week investigation at Haflong, they found that birds surviving the blow will starve to death.

The birds flying to their doom include cattle egrets, white breasted water hens, Bengal florigams, green pigeons, red-breasted parakeets, woodpeckers, red-whiskered bulbul and four species of kingfishers.

It is as though genes of moths had got mixed with genes of birds. No moral to be drawn here, no intimation of anything but chaos and old night. Although there is the perverse detail—that light itself destroys the birds, light domesticated for human use.

*

We look up from a trail in the Santa Ana National Wildlife Refuge, Texas, and see hawks, Broad-winged Hawks, a multitude of Broad-winged Hawks, too many to count, Broad-winged Hawks filling one whole quarter of the sky, with their lazy spirals, Broad-winged Hawks ascending, descending, overwhelming. Overwhelmed, we stare and stare. My wife puts a hand on my arm, I pat the hand. This is a different sense of things: Adam and Eve witnessing for the first time the magnitude of carnivorous beauty, ferocious grace. What a gorgeously uncanny world. (Were we really born on this earth or were we abandoned here before our first memories?)

A gasp, but no words, for words have not yet been given to spectacles like this. Sentences, tidy grammar, these would belie the massive, shifting syntax expressing itself overhead. We hardly dare even point.

At last, we must move on out of the shadow of the hawks, but still we say little. Then we flush a Virginia Rail from a clump of marsh grass and the charm is broken.

Lewis listens to this, pipe in mouth. When I finish, he removes the pipe and stares at it with something like surprise. But he is not seeing the pipe. He is seeing a contradiction in my position.

"But you know, Leonard," he says, "here you are describing an epiphany—I take it that's what you mean to do—in terms of sheer number. And sheer number is a matter of quantity, the very stuff you were so down on the last time we talked. How do you wriggle out of that?"

"Well," I serenely reply, "there are moments when number, if it has sufficient magnitude, becomes quality."

Jamming the pipe into his mouth, Lewis says, "Oh, come on!"

*

Audubon describes the return of the Passenger Pigeons to their roosts on the banks of the Green River in Kentucky:

> As the period of their arrival approached, their foes anxiously prepared to receive them. Some were furnished with iron-pots containing sulphur, others with torches of pine-knots, many with poles, and the rest with guns. The sun was lost to our view, yet not a Pigeon had arrived. Every thing was ready, and all eyes were gazing on the clear sky, which appeared in glimpses amidst the tall trees. Suddenly there burst forth a general cry of "Here they come!" The noise which they

made, though yet distant, reminded me of a hard
gale at sea, passing through the rigging of a close-
reefed vessel. As the birds arrived and passed over
me, I felt a current of air that surprised me. Thousands were soon knocked down by the pole-men.
The birds continued to pour in. The fires were
lighted, and a magnificent, as well as wonderful
and almost terrifying, sight presented itself. The
Pigeons, arriving by thousands, alighted everywhere, one above another, until solid masses as
large as hogsheads were formed on the branches
all round. Here and there the perches gave way
under the weight with a crash, and, falling to the
ground, destroyed hundreds of the birds beneath,
forcing down the dense groups with which every
stick was loaded. It was a scene of uproar and
confusion. I found it quite useless to speak, or
even to shout to those persons who were nearest
to me. Even the reports of the guns were seldom
heard, and I was made aware of the firing only by
seeing the shooters reloading.

No one dared venture within the line of devastation. The hogs had been penned up in due time,
the picking up of the dead and wounded being
left for the next morning's employment. The Pigeons were constantly coming, and it was past
midnight before I perceived a decrease in the
number of those that arrived. . . . The howlings of
the wolves now reached our ears, and the foxes,
lynxes, cougars, bears, raccoons, oppossums and

pole-cats were seen sneaking off, whilst eagles and hawks of different species, accompanied by a crowd of vultures, came to supplant them, and enjoy their share of the spoil.

It was then that the authors of all this devastation began their entry amongst the dead, the dying, and the mangled. The pigeons were picked up and piled in heaps, until each had as many as he could possibly dispose of, when the hogs were let loose to feed on the remainder.

This is the description of a scene in Hell as witnessed by a man who doesn't notice that he is describing Hell.

He continues:

Persons unacquainted with these birds might naturally conclude that such dreadful havock would soon put an end to the species. But I have satisfied myself, by long observation, that nothing but the gradual diminution of our forests can accomplish their decrease, as they not unfrequently quadruple their numbers yearly, and always at least double it. In 1805 I saw schooners loaded in bulk with Pigeons caught up the Hudson River, coming in to the wharf at New York, when the birds sold for a cent a piece. I knew a man in Pennsylvania, who caught and killed upwards of 500 dozens in a clap-net in one day, sweeping sometimes twenty dozens or more at a single haul.

Sheer quantity here darkens the vision of a rational mind. There is no inherent principle in quantity itself to tell us how much, if any, is good or bad. A quota of anything is always arbitrary.

*

The last known individual of the species [Passenger Pigeon], a female named Martha, died in 1914 in the Cincinnati Zoo and is now on display in the U.S. National Museum of Natural History.

*

Obsession finds evidence everywhere—this in Arthur Quinn's *A New World*, regarding the explorer Samuel Champlain:

At times, for the new and marvelous he was willing to risk all, only later to rebuke himself for his irrational behavior. Once he lost contact with his party because he wandered off in pursuit of an extraordinary bird. At least his description of it is extraordinary, for no one has ever seen such a bird in an eastern woodland since. Like an uncanny creature from a fairy tale, it always stayed just out of reach, leading him deeper and deeper into the forest, only then to disappear. And only then, its spell over him broken, did he come to his senses.

By then, realizing that he was utterly lost, he all but despaired of finding his party; but after days of wandering the forest, finally stumbled across them.

> He could then, in safety, berate himself for having behaved like a child, for having succumbed to the bait of novelty. He had actually almost wasted his life in pursuit of pretty plumage, a humbling realization.

This is Champlain's story, but we are under no obligation to draw from it the moral that its hero offers.

*

I read Lewis the passage from Quinn. His reply, "Interesting." This is a term I have noticed often used by scientists to describe any phenomenon, great or small, that seems attractively novel. But when I hear it so used, I cannot help recalling Martin Buber's comment that, to the great artist, the "interesting is not important."

*

Lewis goes out as my guest with Thursday's Children. The group, once they see what a gracious, well-mannered man they have as a companion, exchange a certain wariness for cordial welcome, even pride to have so distinguished a figure be one of them for a day. Lewis makes a friend of Naomi by deferring to her leadership, although she in turn is quick to repay that deference with her own. It is an easy day, none of the birds seen offering any difficulty.

When we break for lunch, Lewis contributes his share to the small talk, with a good story from his Arctic researches. And when the day ends, there are handshakes all around and invitations for him to join the group any time he cares to.

On the way home, he is quiet, responding to my comments with a noncommittal, "Umm." When finally he speaks up, he brushes aside the question I just put as if he hadn't heard it.

"I think you miss something very important. Very important."

"What's that?" I ask.

"Well, you're so preoccupied with the individual experience that you may miss the real center of birdwatching. I mean, the strong glue it provides for bonding individuals who are not all that easy with socializing. I noticed you, Leonard, were not a solitary figure peering into romantic distance for the gleam of real presence. No, you gave as good as you got. We all did, and that giving and taking was, spiced with a good bird or two, the real essence of this activity. Take that elderly couple, the tall, frail man and his sturdy little wife—what's their name?"

"The Murchisons, you mean?"

"Yes, the Murchisons. They strike me as probably very conservative in their ordinary lives, people busy with narrow concerns, not apt to be seen at many parties, theirs or anyone else's. But out here, on nobody's turf, they are almost jolly, when he isn't studying the trees or she isn't studying him to make sure he isn't about to take a header. There's a magic as strong as church that brings them out here—maybe stronger, a magic that can bring opposing creeds together, and left, middle, and right wings."

We are silent till Lewis pulls up at my house. As I open the door to get out, I say, "Sometimes I think of birdwatching as a sort of therapeutic exclusion; we focus on a small object at a distance and literally shut out the rest of the world."

"That," Lewis replies, amused to have found another inconsistency in my thinking, "isn't much support for your notion of epiphany, is it?"

My wife, who has come out to say hello to Lewis, answers for me, "Oh, he doesn't mind. What would he do if the issue were settled?"

*

Someone has left open the kitchen door leading out into the garden. A House Sparrow zooms in through that gap, discovers its progress blocked, and becomes a sudden ball of panic, bouncing off walls, twitching up, twitching down, thrashing the sunny panes with its wings. All our attempts to show it the door merely deepen its fright. Finally, exhausted and dazzled, it comes to rest on a high shelf, pauses there awhile, then, much to our surprise, spreads its wings and, with its dignity only a little ruffled, sails coolly out and back into its own world.

One sparrow in a room reminds me of another, more famous, which appears briefly in a passage from the medieval historian Bede to induce unillumined pagans to heed the call of Christ. This sparrow, "flying in at one door, and immediately out at another, whilst he is within, is safe from the wintry storm; but after a short space of fair weather, he immediately vanishes out of your sight, into the dark winter from which he had emerged. So this life of man. . . ."

Our sparrow offered no obvious moral, only a lucid absence where it had, mysteriously, recovered and composed itself as a particular bird at a particular time in a particular, if wrong, place.

*

David, my poet friend, has taken to sending me material he thinks belongs in my imaginary bird anthology. He seems to have one criterion for his choices: a certain avian nastiness, meant, I presume, to be a curative for any sentimentality I might be developing toward birds. The latest he has fetched up from Virgil's *Aeneid*, a description of the dreadful Harpies:

> No monster more noxious than these, no crueller
> plague or fury of the gods ever arose
> from Stygian waves. These birds wear virgin faces,
> but their bellies leak a vile filth,
> their hands are claws, their features always pale
> with ravenous hunger.

These hideous birds with their innocent girl faces are a brilliant oxymoronic invention, of a time that probably had not yet developed an abstract language for the messy contradictions inherent in life.

I'm grateful to David, even though he meant only to disgust me.

*

I dream my sacred book. Slowly I turn its glowing pages— too much to choose from! I stop briefly at "The Tale of the Nightingale King" but know it's not what I'm looking for. What I'm looking for is this, my Italian traveler:

On business in the city of Cremona, at the inn where he was lodged, Stampari met a man who claimed to have invented an artificial bird so like a living one that if you came upon it not knowing its true progenitor, you might think it hatched from the egg of an actual bird. When Stampari asked the inventor if he could see this marvel, the man waved his arms, frowned, and behaved so uneasily that the traveler concluded that he was mad or drunk. Glad he had business on the other side of town, Stampari excused himself and hurried off, thinking no more of the matter. Imagine then his surprise when he returned to his lodgings and found a message awaiting him that he was to present himself by eight sharp at 6 Via de Sale, the house in which the inventor had his studio, and there he would be fully satisfied as to the truth of what he had heard.

Nothing could keep Stampari from accepting this invitation and promptly at eight he appeared at the address he was given and banged the brass knocker of the thick oak door. A man so old he seemed ageless opened the door and, after looking the visitor up and down, made a gesture for him to enter, took his hat and coat, and beckoned Stampari to follow him down an ill-lit hall past several rooms, their doors shut. Behind one were voices of muffled anger; behind another, music picked out note by note on a clavicembalo with a melancholy effect. Behind a third, a child was sobbing. Finally, the servant stopped in front of a door from behind which came an exquisite warbling. Suddenly the door flew open and there stood his host, a finger to his lips, his gaze on a huge cage that occupied much of the room. Stampari followed the man's eyes and beheld the bird perched on a little swing suspended from the top of the cage.

He writes that the bird was indeed handsomely

wrought, its feathers an elegant balance of black and white, its shape pleasantly rounded. The inventor, obviously proud of his work, smiled and invited his guest to come closer, saying very softly, "Perhaps, *signore*, you can, with your sharp eyes, detect traces of the maker's hand?"

Stampari looked closely, but could find nothing that betrayed the artificiality of the bird.

"No?" said his host. "Well, then, I will give you a little hint. Note the eye, *signore*. Note that the look comes, as it were, from nowhere, has no source."

Stampari studied the eye and had to admit, yes, that seemed to be the case. Just then the bird fluttered up from the perch and flew around the inside of the cage three times, then resumed its perch and commenced singing.

"You will surely have noticed, *signore*, that, although it flies like an angel, I still have not solved the problem of a certain mechanical repetition of its flight. If you were to stay here for several hours, you would see what I mean. Always the same flutter up, the same three circles, then back on the perch to sing again." He shook his head and sighed.

Stampari, feeling that the man was being too modest, complimented him on his artistry, his genius; but the man became gloomier and gloomier and kept saying, "Next time, next time, I will do it right. I have half a mind to throw this poor child into the trash."

Stampari tried to argue him out of his gloom, to no avail. The man grew excited and shook his fist at his creation, then snatched up a net leaning against the cage.

"What are you going to do?" Stampari said, alarmed at the man's violence.

"You will see," was the reply.

"Wait!" cried Stampari. "I will buy the bird from you. Yes, I will buy it!"

"Nonsense!" shouted his host. "It is unworthy of your interest, let alone your money."

"Let me be the judge of that," his guest shouted back. "Here." Stampari reached in his pocket and fished out a considerable number of gold coins. His host waved them away. But finally, after much beseeching, he relented and agreed to the purchase. He stepped into the cage and, after some trouble, netted the bird, took it to a little corner table, did something to it, then put it in a small cage that could be carried by hand. It now seemed droopy, squatting on the cage's bottom.

"I have stilled it by pressing this little button—ah, you can't see it because it is hidden by the wing. Note where it is, for it will be necessary to press it when you wish the bird to fly and sing again."

Then he put a cover on the cage, handed it to Stampari, and now seemed anxious to be rid of his guest. He took him by the arm and, muttering excuses, ushered Stampari out of the room; the old servant escorted him again past the closed doors—behind which now reigned a total silence—handed him his hat and coat, and sent him into the night.

As he drew near his lodgings, Stampari began to feel—

what? That he had just been tested and found wanting. By the time he had climbed the stairs to his room, he was certain that he had been lured into behavior that was, for a man of his acuity, stupid. Once in his room, he set the cage down on the table next to his bed but did not yet remove the cover. Suddenly, it came to him: All that had just transpired had been a theatrical performance—the ancient servant, the sounds of pathos from behind the shut doors, the dramatic introduction to the bird. All these, yes, had been *calculated* to make him feel the unreality of the situation, each thing a signal to treat what was happening as fragile appearance, ready to burst like a bubble with the first pinprick of reason.

But why? Why was he brought, step by step, to feel this? There was only one answer. The bird was—and here he swept the covering off the cage—real! And indeed it was, poor thing, languishing on the cage floor, likely drugged. And so he had been fooled by a master of illusion, so much a master that he was able to make what was real seem false, even make the real participate in the illusion that it wasn't.

It would have been pointless to return to the house. The illusionist by now would have vanished, his pocket full of gold coins, his pride soaring. As for Stampari, he tells us that he sat there a long while, enraged but also full of admiration. The poor bird, meanwhile, expired. When, later, he described the creature to a friend, who knew about such things, he learned that it was no Italian bird, but probably one from the far north. As Stampari made to leave, his friend, grinning, said, "My dear fellow, appearance is also real."

*

It's raining rain and warblers on High Island, Texas. Hundreds of birds fall out of the sky and alight in the pecan trees. A storm has blocked their northward migration, exhausted them, until they are forced to land. "Fallout," it's called. So their misfortune is our great luck. Up go the binoculars—and there the warblers are in their spring plumage: Cerulean, Cape May, Chestnut-sided, Blackburnian, Magnolia, Blue-winged, Golden-winged, Bay-breasted.

It's wonderful, but too much for me. I swing my binoculars right and left, torn between this or that bird. I feel that I am not seeing nearly all there is to see, and if what I see is wonderful, what I don't see distracts me. "To offer immensities to one who asks a small favor is a kind of refusal." But Petrarch's shrewd observation doesn't really apply to me. I've asked for immensities simply by being here. Asked for immensities but am unable to receive them.

As always when I bounce off one of my limits, when my eyes prove far less keen than my appetite, I am saddened. A feeling of failure is as palpable as the rain that pelts me even while I focus on a Blackburnian's brilliant orange and black. I ought to be grateful. I *am* grateful. And moved. But I am also disappointed. Disappointment follows me around all day like a second, darker shadow.

Are the strangers shouting their joy on either side of me also secret sharers of a double mood? I don't dare ask for fear they are. Or worse, for fear they are not.

*

We have been sitting silent in the manner of old friends who don't need to keep the conversational ball forever in the air.

We are letting dusk happen, that unworldly time between light and dark, the poet's hour, Lewis calls it, "when the deceiving specters of ambiguity are set loose and can lead us to believe the impossible." Nevertheless, Lewis likes this time as much as I do.

We have been talking about my adventures at High Island and my contradictory feelings as the warblers landed in the pecans. But talking about the experience somehow takes much of the joy and sadness out of it, and I sound to myself like someone indulging pathos for its own sake. Lewis surprises me. Instead of jumping on this opportunity, he nods, seeming to sympathize. And now we both have become quiet.

The only sound comes from outside—the call of a Mourning Dove, perhaps just before settling in for the night.

Lewis breaks the stillness, his voice coming from darkness: "Such stories, of course, can give our lives shape and purpose, but yours, Leonard"—and here he laughs, not without affection—"yours can sometimes resemble a comedy, the hero bisected into Dr. Manic and Mr. Depressive, who spend most of their time batting each other around with various kitchen implements."

"And your story, Lewis?"

A long pause, then the bodiless voice from darkness: "Oh, you know I never tell stories."

*

Thursday's Children stand by their scopes on a windy cliff edge. Thirty feet below, black breakers slam into red, offshore rocks, raising fountains of foam and spray. When the waters recede, large surfaces of the rocks are exposed. We intently watch these surfaces and have so far spotted oystercatchers, Surfbirds, Rock Sandpipers, Lesser Yellowlegs, Black Turnstones, as well as pelicans, cormorants, and assorted gulls.

Uneasy on high places, I locate myself a little back from the cliff edge. As I peer through my scope, I become aware of someone standing beside me. I look up to find it is Naomi's visitor from the Midwest, Gillian, a pleasant, quiet, middle-aged woman.

"Naomi tells me you're writing a book about birdwatching." As she says this, she blushes. And I blush with her, as if it were an embarrassment to discuss such things in public. We smile encouragingly at each other and she continues, "Naomi says you think it's . . . a religious experience."

"Well," I say, a little alarmed, "not quite that, though *like* that."

But she is following her own thoughts now, her gaze fixed on the water, her eyes shining. "I have believed that for years." Here she looks at me and says with easy politeness, "I do so look forward to reading your book—when it comes out."

I am about to thank her when someone spots Sooty Shearwaters at two o'clock going left, their elegant, tilted flight carrying them fast and low in the troughs of the waves. I get them in my scope, then turn to offer Gillian a look. But she is now standing beside Naomi. We don't speak again except for exchanging good-byes at day's end. As we do so, I blush again. Gillian doesn't. Perhaps I should have ignored the shearwaters and turned the scope on this stranger whom I never quite got into focus.

*

"And," my wife says as we leave the restaurant, "what comes after the Snow Bunting?"

It's a brilliantly clear night full of shapely constellations, a night for honest answers. "Haven't the faintest notion," I say, opening the car door for her.

When I go around and climb in behind the wheel, she adds, "I wonder if one can retire an obsession?"

*

I put myself to sleep by reciting all the birds I can recall that poets have put in their poems. There are so many kinds from albatross to wren, some of swanlike beauty, others homely as crows. The air is full of them and they keep coming. It only adds to their presence that they are silent in my imagined sky. The Snow Bunting is up there among them, between skylark and swallow.

But besides flight—and not all birds fly—what do they share, these poetic birds? Perhaps, and without ever knowing it, only this: the heavy burden of human cares and hopes.

I repeat over and over, "The heavy burden of human cares and hopes," a chant that carries me into sleep, into a dream of pursuit, in which I run and run like some prehistoric stick figure daubed on a cave wall. I run tirelessly, timelessly right out into morning and the sweet if brief amnesia of waking.

*

I've been neglecting my imaginary anthology. Then two Red-tailed Hawks dancing around each other in the sky remind me of Whitman's "The Dalliance of the Eagles," a little worn with use, yes, but perhaps worth a fresh look:

Skirting the river road, (my forenoon walk, my rest,)
Skyward in air a sudden muffled sound, the dalliance of the
    eagles,
The rushing amorous contact high in space together,
The clinching interlocking claws, a living, fierce, gyrating
    wheel,
Four beating wings, two beaks, a swirling mass tight
    grappling,
In tumbling turning clustering loops, straight downward
    falling,
Till o'er the river pois'd, the twain yet one, a moment's lull,
A motionless still balance in the air, then parting, talons
    loosing,
Upward again on slow-firm pinions slanting, their separate
    diverse flight,
She hers, he his, pursuing.

I had never noticed before, or noticed but forgot, the tact and modesty Whitman exercises here. He, who could with such consummate ease assume the role of mentor or prophet, offers us only the event itself with no editorializing. It's a fine restraint that, as far as possible, lets the birds be birds, lets them mean and act in their own right by their own laws. The power and grace of their high actions are all the more powerful, graceful, by their independence from the casual observer, who wants nothing but to see them as they are.

*

Morning and a bird sings out back. I instantly sit up, but it takes time to separate what belongs to sleep from what belongs to waking. Now the song clarifies—two slurry notes, two higher, then a long, tumbling trill downward. I don't recognize it—warbler? sparrow? More like a sparrow. My wife drowsily asks, "What is it?" I shrug, slip out of bed, get my binoculars, and peer out a back window. The song has now stopped. All I hear is the ratchety call of the Steller's Jay perched on the top of the highest birch.

It seems the mystery bird has flown on to offer someone readier the chance to give it its name. Which is worse—to be deaf or to hear but not recognize?

After breakfast, I go through the field guides, but no luck. And now I'm not quite sure about what I heard. Memory, given some time, can edit, can add a note here, subtract one there, lengthen or shorten, speed or slow. I give up, surrender the bird to oblivion, and get down to business. Which is to write about birdwatching.

I begin: "Morning and a bird sings out back." This time perhaps.

*

Lewis stoops to pick up a red-tinged feather lying on the path. He tells me that it belonged to a flicker, points out some of its features—rachis, vanes, calamus—then, giving it to me, says that I now hold in the palm of my hand a natural miracle.

So light is it that, if I turn my eyes away, I will know it's there only because of a sensation of softness. It's all grace in and of itself. But the license I permit myself I won't permit Lewis, and I say, "If you mean by miracle the suspension of natural law, isn't that a contradiction?"

Lewis shrugs and says, rather brusquely, "Forget that. That's small potatoes. The serious miracle is that there is law at all."

I stare hard at my friend. He stares hard at the distance, but not like a man who expects anything new on the horizon.

*

Saint Francis, at the end, was surrounded by larks, his favorites because they were outwardly drab, cowled like monks, and, like monks, ate humbly what the earth gave, and risen, praised the Lord in their song.

So it happened that after vespers, late on the Sabbath, a great company of these little birds descended on the house in which he lay. They circled above the roof, singing their hearts out and "seemed likewise to praise the Lord." I worry about the word "seemed"—does it concede too much to doubt, to commonplace skepticism?—then I recall the words of Stampari's friend: "My dear fellow, appearance is also real."

＊

"I used to keep lists, but not anymore," she says, the tall, soft-voiced young woman who has fallen in with Thursday's Children and now walks beside me toward the cypresses where warblers were seen this morning. "I guess I'm not a birder," she says.

"A birdwatcher perhaps," I suggest.

"Yes," she says, "but more likely just a curious person who'll stop for anything that catches her eye."

We laugh and go silent for a bit. Then she says, "I have a sort of confession to make."

"Oh?" I say.

"Yes. I watched your group as they came down from the upper trail, and it was—oh my—I can't find the word. Well, haunting. That's not right either, but you know, it was such a quiet and solemn procession, as if you were performing some ceremony. I know it sounds weird to say so, but I wouldn't have been very surprised if you had started to chant. Do you know what I mean?"

"I think I do," I say, "but I wouldn't tell all this to a serious birder."

Again we laugh and go silent. Then she says, "Your binoculars even added to the effect—all of you carrying them over your breasts, like a symbol for something. Does that sound silly?"

"Not at all," I say and would like to hug her.

"Before you got here," she says, "another group was out at the cypresses and I was watching them, when I turned suddenly and saw up in the branches a Great Horned Owl watching *me*! Isn't that amazing? I wanted to shout at the group, tell them what a wonder they were missing. But I'm not much of a shouter and they probably would have thought I was crazy."

"Far from crazy," I say, as Claire comes abreast of us and the conversation takes a new turn.

*

It's like a Chinese ink drawing—pine forest and a few roofs on a mountain half-hidden in mist that feels "around / for a home it will never find." Color is subdued to black, gray, moss-darkened green. And silence. The only motion: three Great Egrets gliding by in their hunched flight. I have seen egrets too many times to count, but these seem utterly fresh and vivid.

It's like an ink drawing except that I'm in it. And in it, I require nothing else but to be in it. Now a thrush sings its upward-circling quaver, and what seemed perfect before seems more so now. And then a human voice calls from somewhere behind me, and I am fetched, unwilling, back to the other world.

*

Once when my wife went out watching with me, she elected to stay by the car while I hiked about three hundred yards out over a big, newly plowed field. When I reached the far edge of it, I turned around and, lifting my binoculars to my eyes, looked at my wife who was just then looking at me through her binoculars. Strange familiars. Familiar strangers. I blew her a kiss. She waved at me.

*

Very carefully, Lewis lifts the filled feeder onto the hook and lets it go. It sways only a little. "I swear," he grumbles, "that squirrel's an Einstein among his brethren. He's managed to get past every obstacle I've put in his way."

We are sipping sherry in the shade of the copper beech that dominates Lewis's backyard. We have of course been talking about talking about birds, Lewis arguing that I still didn't appreciate the spare and gritty elegance of the field report. Didn't see how beautifully suited its language was for the experience it was designed to keep track of, how its refusal to moralize or elicit pathos exactly mirrored the natural world it aimed to comprehend. "In any case," he says, "it does the job."

"But, Lewis," I protest, "that leaves us with a sense of a world as desiccated, as alien to us as Mars, a matter of dry data, patterns of abstract behavior all reducible to pure number. There's so much more that gets left out—the whole feel of things."

"Oh, I leave that to you poets, so long as it's understood that, whatever you say about it can only be subjectively true, a matter of strongly felt opinion at best, at worst, downright error. Everybody knows, except the poets, that it's the male nightingale that does the singing. If you get the wrong sex of real presence, how real is it and what's your epiphany worth then? Or your reverence? I'll take Tinbergen's little study of the Snow Bunting—the one that so bored you—over any number of subjective impressions, however prettily presented. And not just because studies like Tinbergen's have a chance to be true, but because they also have their own kind of excitement, an excitement you are evidently blind to."

"I admit it. Any excitement I felt in reading it came from my trying to imagine myself there."

"Well, that's not the worst way to start, if you remember that you can't be there as a freelance adventurer, extracting what you imagine is some essence from the experience, then flying off to a warm study to record your feelings about it. I've told you before: Field study requires hard labor, a willingness to sit a whole bitterly cold day on some icy ridge waiting for something to happen. But the willingness and waiting sometimes pay off with a special thrill.

You feel it when you see knowledge—even small bits of it—fill in the empty slots of your ignorance, when data begin to assemble themselves into a pattern."

"I think I can see that," I say, "even if the thrill is forever beyond me. What I insist, though, is that this thrill of yours is the result of pushing your experience more and more toward the abstract, toward birds as an example of race, species, genus, ultimately as confirmation of natural law. Your language is constituted to do that. But there's another language, dedicated to articulating the sense or feel of an experience. In order to perform that task, it must sometimes break with straightforward language, resort to violations of grammar, syntax, and logic; it must exploit devices like hyperbole, understatement, paradox, oxymoron, irony, strong patterns of meter and rhyme—all the devices of all writers who have undertaken to summon forth and record the most difficult of all things to express: the living presence."

"A very pretty speech, Leonard, but I'll wager that any group of intelligent, educated men and women, offered a choice between your language and mine as a way to a truth that would save their lives, would choose mine without the slightest hesitation."

"Lewis," I say, "could I have another sherry?" But his attention now is all on a squirrel seated on the back fence not twenty feet from where we sit. It watches us intently as though it were listening to our debate with great interest. A third point of view?

*

When I walked to Lewis's, it was sunny. Now a thick fog has rolled in and, walking home, I remember walking home through the chilling air of another autumn in another town. On that day, as I turned the corner to my street, I looked up into the broad sycamore I was just then passing under and saw there hundreds of blackbirds sitting utterly still. I ducked my head, hurried my pace, and was relieved to find home where I had left it that morning, nothing bad having happened, a good blaze in the fireplace and a hot drink held out.

*

I dream the sacred book open to a page with this written across it: *Stampari settentrionàle.* On the next page, I find Stampari in London at the residence of a fellow Italian, a scholar brought to England as tutor to the son of a great lord. Among the other guests this evening was a ship's captain, a Dane, one Haakon, a man Stampari found charming and widely read in the classics. The captain was plainly taken with the Italian and, made liberal by strong spirits, invited Stampari to be his guest on a voyage to Bergen, where Haakon was to deliver a cargo of English wool. Stampari, also emboldened by spirits, readily accepted, forgetting even to ask the date of sailing. Next morning, he received a note confirming in the strongest terms the invitation and instructing him to be with his gear at such-and-such a dock at exactly half past five the next morning when the vessel, the *Raven*, would catch a favorable tide. Headache and second thoughts notwithstanding, there he was on said dock at the appointed hour, his gear around him, his gaze on the vessel moored there, a merchantman sitting low in the water and painted white with black trim.

Not a scholar of naval matters, Stampari knew enough to recognize the kind of craft in which he would reside for a while, no winged creature, but a cog, a slow, broadwaisted ship, its stern and stem bluntly snubbed.

Once aboard he was welcomed by Haakon, but the captain was so busy that Stampari spent his first hour alone, dodging sailors trying to perform their duties in small, crowded quarters. Finally, he and his gear were taken to his cabin, a tiny space to be shared with the first mate, a tall, taciturn, red-haired Norwegian named Thorvald.

Once the vessel was under way, Stampari went out on deck and was shown around, on the captain's instructions, by this same Thorvald. By the time the *Raven* reached open waters, the passenger felt almost at home, although the sea was rougher than the river had been and he was forced to don a warm coat in the face of a brisk, chilly wind from the northeast. It was to avoid the wind's full force that the captain took the boat toward the coast of Norway.

Stampari was a fair sailor, untroubled by rocking ships, but as the days passed he did find himself more than a little bored. The coast might have offered the gaze a certain grandeur but it was hidden at first in mist, then by snowfall. The wind now increased, blowing the vessel off course, to the northwest. It seemed there was precious little that could be done about it in the midst of what now was a blinding blizzard. Whereas on the first few nights Stampari had enjoyed dinner and conversation with the captain and one or more the mates, all now were too busy for such leisure; and the vessel, buffeted by heavy seas, ceased to be comfortable. And Stampari now began to experience some queasiness, a promise of things to come.

Over the next days, matters got worse — the sea rougher, the snowfall thicker, the cold more bitter. The captain, an energetic and experienced seaman, did all he could, but from his worried look, it was clear matters were largely out of human hands and there was nothing to do but wait and remain alert, changing or adjusting sails as seemed helpful. There were terrible moments for Stampari, a man from the warm south with its vineyards and olive groves. Shut up in his tiny stifling cabin, he felt that he would never escape this vast all-swallowing zone of whiteness, which gave everything it touched its own pallor. In one such moment, the door flew open and Thorvald, his beard glazed with ice, stumbled in, shouting, "Land! Land!"

Indeed there was a landfall to larboard and they steered toward it, if only to get it between them and the wind; but as they crossed its coast, an opening appeared and they steered for that. In half an hour, they were through it and into calmer waters. Suddenly the wind abated, the blizzard thinned, and they dropped anchor in a relatively sheltered cove. Stampari and the whole crew gave a cheer, although the shore of the haven was bleak.

A boat was lowered into the water, and ten crew members, as well as the guest, set out for that shore, mainly to have a look about, but not expecting much. The party landed and spread out over the landscape, Stampari to the northeast toward the high hills that helped to weaken the force of the storm. He was a little way up the nearest slope when he stopped to fetch his breath and saw coming down on him from the top of the hill a cloud, a very strange cloud, moving far more swiftly than an ordinary cloud, and showing in its fleecy white, tiny dark specks. It was now almost overhead and it was *singing.* He was certain he heard a melodic tinkling coming from its swift-moving mass. And now he saw it was indeed no usual cloud, but a cloud of birds, hundreds sweeping over his head and down toward the shore, out over the bay and the vessel, and then, in a wide arc to the right, circling back to land, curving round to where he stood watching it pass up and over the hill—*straordinàrio*!

Back on board the *Raven*, he rushed to tell Haakon, but the captain, who was standing with Thorvald, surveying the damage done by the blizzard, forestalled him with a gesture, "I also saw, my friend."

"But what, what?" asked Stampari.

"They are called by the sailors 'Snowflakes'; in your language, I believe, *fiòcco di néve.*"

And then it came to Stampari—these birds were the

very same as the "mechanical" bird he had purchased in Cremona. For no obvious reason, his heart began to beat fast, and he had the eerie sensation of being in two places at once, like a man separated from himself, or from his fate. His face burned. An intense buzzing in his head deadened the captain's words and all he remembered from that moment was the look of alarm on his friend's face.

The story seems to end here, except that on a final page there is this: "How much real, how much fever phantom?" And, below this, in another's hand: "No record of Stampari's ever having been in Bergen, or for that matter, in London."

*

A picture of the Snow Bunting lies open before me on my desk. I have been trying hard to see it without imposing on it an aura of human meaning. But I can't help finding in its black-and-white symmetries an eloquence that goes beyond biological purpose, a superfluous beauty. And I realize that, even were I never to see an actual bird whole and clear in its spring plumage, my heart in hiding will have been stirred, briefly awakened to an intense reality in the fluttery glimpse I got through the cold air of Cape Merry. Not an epiphany perhaps, but something very like, which surprised my attention and was, after all, not wholly lost on me.

*

Another black-and-white symmetry: Robert Frost's brief "Dust of Snow":

> The way a crow
> Shook down on me
> The dust of snow
> From a hemlock tree
>
> Has given my heart
> A change of mood
> And saved some part
> Of a day I had rued.

And yet another such symmetry on a just-arrived postcard: "You'll say Emily Dickinson — and be wrong:

> I saw a single Blackbird
> perched on a whitened Bough,
> Its Feathers, draggled Ensigns —
> Defiant of the snow —
>
> Encounter without Strings,
> Or doubtful Questions — why? —
> Remindful that We had,
> Permission yet to Fly —"

On the picture side is a splendid Indian pigeon, the Pied Imperial, whose black-and-white pattern makes it seem like a pigeonized version of a Snow Bunting, as my friend, no doubt smiling, well knew when he plucked the card from the tray, smiling even more when he saw how the scheme of black and white is carried into the bird and snow of the poem — so that everything on the card (except the stamp) rhymed.

I return the favor in the next mailing: "Not quite Emily but a better than fair mockingbird."

*

"That's it! That's it!" We see it in the same instant. It's perched with a watchful intentness on a bare twig in the middle of an Arizona pecan orchard. No doubt about it: brilliant red head and undersides, dark tail and back, and broad eye line. I think I can even see the whiskers at the base of the beak.

This is my first Vermilion Flycatcher, a fine adult male. My wife turns and smiles a smile that at first I think means she's glad for me. But it's too broad for that. She has seen, and seeing, seen beyond mere seeing.

We watch our bird for a while. Every so often, he flits up, zigs, banks, snatches an insect out of the air, then returns to the same perch. Sometimes he flies hard at an immature male who veers too close to his kingdom. His redness glows like a palpable force.

All the way back to the city, I feel happily companionable, wanting to be close to my fellow seer. But I also feel a little aloof as if something in the experience can't be shared except in the experiencing.

Does she have the same feelings? Why can't I ask her?

*

A beautiful winter photograph of a Northern Cardinal perched on a berry bush whose scarlet fruit is coated by ice. The bird gazes forever at this saving morsel forever locked away from it and will never see spring again—the price of the immortality conferred by art.

*

Thursday's Children, eating lunch now, have had a good morning—a very rare Little Curlew the prize. We are expansive and talk about things we might ordinarily keep back. We play a mild game of confession: What is the bird each of us would most like to see and why? When it comes my turn, unsurprisingly, I bring up the Snow Bunting, no special wonder for most of the group and known to be my odd obsession, an occasion for good-humored teasing.

"If you're so hellbent on seeing that bird," Spencer says, "why don't you get on one of those Alaskan tours and damn well see it?" Spencer is a man who believes that the shortest distance between two points is a straight line; and more, that the shortest distance is invariably the preferable one.

In most instances I would agree with Spencer on this point. I try to explain that hopping on a plane, hopping off, seeing the bird, hopping back on, would take something essential out of the experience, a sense of discovery, of risk, of—I don't quite know what but know that it is a necessary ingredient to the seeing I cherish. There must, I argue, be an element of surprise in it.

I don't mention epiphany or intimation or reverence because, for Spencer, such terms mean nothing beyond their vaguely religious association and carry less weight with him, who has long ago left the church, than do the axioms of structural engineering.

I try to find an analogy he will buy. "It would be like going to see the bird in an aviary or in a refuge that restricted its movements."

Spencer shrugs. He isn't buying. "When I saw the bird, about ten years back, I just hopped off a plane and the sky didn't fall in."

"Not *my* bird!" I say to myself.

Spencer, clapping me on the shoulder, says, "You're going to be so hot and bothered when you get your big chance, all you'll see is the steam on your binoculars." Everyone laughs. Then, Spencer surprises me, saying very softly, "Listen, I think I know what you mean."

I thank Spencer but wonder if his meaning and mine are simply two separate species perched a moment on the same bush.

*

I wake from a long, elaborate, allegorical dream, remembering only this: I meet a man going the other way. We sweep our hats off and bow.

"Stampari," I say, "farewell. For now."
That's all, and this feeling of sober expectancy.

*

Lewis will be having dinner with us tonight, bringing with him a copy of his new book. The champagne is chilling, the ingredients for dinner all set out in order: olive oil, tomato, tomato paste, garlic, chives, arugula, tarragon, peppercorns, polenta. I'm in good spirits, my own book almost done, although I don't know how it will end or, more precisely, how to end it. My wife is arranging a bunch of bright orange alstroemeria in a royal blue vase. She is humming to herself.

I wave a piece of paper and she smiles and sits down. I clear my throat and read:

> Silhouette of a small bird
> on a telephone wire at twilight,
> singing a soft and shaky song,
> song, I think, of the too late,
> a too late song. Listen—

The ring of the doorbell interrupts.

*

I'm flying. North.

As we were about to leave for the airport, the mailman handed me one item—a postcard. On its picture side was a Boreal Owl, one eye open. On the other side, from the Book of Mark:

"And what I say unto you I say unto all, Watch."

*

REFERENCES

PAGE 3

The Analects of Confucius, Arthur Waley, trans. Book XVII. London: Allen & Unwin, 1949.

PAGES 11–12

Peattie, Donald Culross, *Singing in the Wilderness: A Salute to John James Audubon.* New York: G. P. Putnam's Sons, 1935.

PAGE 17

Wordsworth, William. *The Prelude.* Book Eleven. New York/ Toronto: Rinehart & Co., Inc., 1948.

PAGE 18

Dennis, Carl. "The Bird Watcher." *Signs and Wonders.* Princeton, NJ: Princeton University Press, 1979.

PAGE 22

Ruskin, John. *The Stones of Venice.* New York: Hill and Wang, 1960.

PAGE 22

Ellis, Havelock. *The Dance of Life.* New York: Book League of America, 1929.

PAGE 22

Goethe, Johann Wolfgang von. *Conversations with Eckermann.* Washington, D.C.: M. W. Dunne, 1901.

PAGES 23, 82

Nethersole-Thompson, Desmond. *The Snow Bunting.* London: Oliver & Boyd Ltd., 1966.

PAGE 24

Pavlich, Walter. "A Theory of Birds." *Running near the End of the World.* Iowa City: University of Iowa Press, 1992.

PAGE 25

Burroughs, John. *Birds and Poets.* Cambridge: The Riverside Press, 1877.

PAGES 39–40

Coleridge, Samuel Taylor. *Anima Poetae.* London: William Heineman, 1895.

PAGES 42–43

Audubon, John James. *Audubon's Birds of America.* Introduction and descriptive captions by Ludlow Griscom. New York: The Macmillan Company, 1950.

PAGE 43

Eiseley, Loren. *The Immense Journey.* New York: Vintage Books, 1951.

PAGE 45

Saint Francis of Assisi. *Considerations on the Stigmata.* Serge Hughs, trans. New York: The New American Library, 1964.

PAGES 48–49

Buber, Martin. *Tales of the Hassidim: The Early Masters.* New York: Schocken Books, 1961.

PAGES 51–52

Hudson, W. H. *Birds and Man.* New York: Alfred A. Knopf, 1923.

PAGE 52

Audubon, John James. *The Birds of America from Drawings Made in the United States and Their Territories.* New York: George R. Lockwood and Son, 1870.

PAGE 52

Harrison, J. E. *Themis: A Study of the Social Origins of Greek Religion.* Cambridge: Cambridge University Press, 1927.

PAGES 54–55

Prescott, William H. *Mexico and the Life of the Conqueror Fernando Cortez.* New York: Peter Fenelon Collier, 1898

PAGES 56, 88

Steiner, George. *Real Presences.* Chicago: University of Chicago Press, 1989.

PAGE 86

Stafford, William. "The View from Here." *Traveling through the Dark.* New York: Harper & Row, 1962.

PAGES 87–88

Jacobsen, Rolf. "Nightbird." *The Silence Afterwards.* Roger Greenwald, trans. Princeton, NJ: Princeton University Press, 1985.

PAGE 94

Auden, W. H. *The Dyer's Hand and Other Essays.* New York: Random House, 1948.

PAGE 95

Gorky, Maxim. *Reminiscences of Tolstoy, Chekhov and Andreev.* S. S. Koteliansky with L.W. and Katherine Mansfield, trans. London: Chatto and Windus, 1994.

PAGES 98–99

Thorburn, Archibald. *British Birds.* New York: Longmans, Green and Co., 1925.

PAGE 100

United Press International. *San Francisco Chronicle.* 22 September 1981.

PAGES 102–104

Audubon, John James. *Audubon Reader.* Scott Russell Sanders, ed. Bloomington: Indiana University Press, 1986.

PAGE 105

Ehrlich, Paul R., and Dobkin, David S., and Wheye, Darryl. *The Birder's Handbook.* New York: Simon & Schuster, 1988.

PAGES 105–106

Quinn, Arthur. *A New World.* Boston: Faber and Faber, Inc., 1994.

PAGE 133

Frost, Robert. *The Poetry of Robert Frost.* Edward Connery Lathem, ed. New York: Henry Holt and Co., Inc., 1923, 1969.

ACKNOWLEDGMENTS

Grateful acknowledgment is made to the following
publications in which the material below first appeared.

Portions of this book have appeared in *California Monthly*,
February 1995 and also in *Mānoa*, Winter 1995.

Auden, W. H. *The Dyer's Hand and Other Essays.* Random
House, Inc. Copyright © 1948, 1950, 1952, 1953, 1956, 1957, 1958,
1960, 1962 by W. H. Auden. Reprinted with the permission of
Random House, Inc.

Buber, Martin. *Tales of the Hassidim: The Early Masters.*
Schocken Books. Copyright © 1961 by Martin Buber. Reprinted
with the permission of Random House, Inc.

Dennis, Carl. *Signs and Wonders.* Princeton University Press.
Copyright © 1979 by Princeton University Press. Reprinted
with the permission of Princeton University Press.

Ehrlich, Paul R., David S. Dobkin, and Darryl Wheye. *The
Birder's Handbook.* Simon & Schuster. Copyright © 1988 by
Paul R. Ehrlich, David S. Dobkin, and Darryl Wheye. Reprinted
with the permission of Simon & Schuster.

Eiseley, Loren. *The Immense Journey.* Vintage Books. Copyright
© 1951 by Loren Eiseley. Reprinted with the permission of Random House, Inc.

Gorky, Maxim. *Reminiscences of Tolstoy, Chekhov and Andreev.*
S. S. Koteliansky and L. W. and Katherine Mansfield, trans.
Chatto & Windus. Copyright © 1994 by Chatto & Windus.
Reprinted with the permission of the Translator's Literary Es-
tate and Chatto & Windus.

LEONARD NATHAN was born in Los Angeles in 1924, served in the U.S. Army during World War II, and finished his B.A., M.A., and Ph.D. at the University of California, Berkeley. He taught in the Department of Rhetoric at Berkeley from 1961 to his retirement in 1991. In addition to receiving many awards and honors, Nathan's book *Returning Your Call* was nominated for a National Book Award, and Nathan is the recipient of the National Institute of Arts and Letters prize for poetry and a Guggenheim Fellowship. Following his retirement, he taught at Stanford University in the Wallace Stegner Poetry Fellowship Program, and has since traveled extensively, mostly as a birdwatcher. Nathan lives in Kensington, California. He has been married for forty-seven years and has three children.

This book was designed by Will Powers.
It is set in Minion and Rusticana
by Stanton Publication Services, Inc.
and manufactured by Quebecor-Fairfield
on acid-free paper.
Cover design by Julie Metz.